Books by Crissy Smith

Were Chronicles

Pack Alpha
Pack Enforcer
Pack Territory
Pack Rogue
Pack Community
Pack Mates
Pack Daughter
Pack Hunter
Pack Council
Pack Security
Pack Beta
Pack Secrets
Pack Balance
Pack Investigator
Pack Law

I0684336

Corporate Wolves

The Favour
Losing Control

Secrets

The Shifter and the Dreamer

Shifter Chronicles

Birds of Prey
Bear Claw
Eye of the Tiger

Coyote's Kiss
Wolf Pack

Bloodlines

Bite
Control

Bite Me!

Savage Love

Summer Seductions

Summers' Girl

Cloaks and Daggers

Vampire Hunter

Lust Bites

Seduced by the Neighbour
Fated Love
Bid High
Lacey's Seduction

What's Her Secret?

What's Her Secret?
Designated Alpha
Last Call

Single Titles

Eternal
Magical Ménage
Vamps in the City

Pack Territory

ISBN # 978-1-78686-123-8

©Copyright Crissy Smith 2017

Cover Art by Posh Gosh ©Copyright 2017

Interior text design by Claire Siemaszkiewicz

Totally Bound Publishing

Published in 2017 by Totally Bound Publishing, Newland House, The Point, Weaver Road, Lincoln, LN6 3QN, United Kingdom.

Totally Bound Publishing is a subsidiary of Totally Entwined Group Limited.

Were Chronicles

PACK TERRITORY

CRISSY SMITH

Dedication

This book is dedicated to everyone looking for their home and family. It's not only blood that matters, but a home and family by choice is just as important. Be yourself and love yourself first.

Chapter One

The wind blew so hard Adam White could feel it rustling his fur even as he stood still. He ignored the strong breeze to remain staring down on his territory. Adam felt the deep connection to the land and knew he'd do anything to bring his Pack back together.

The stress of an attack several months ago that had almost killed one of the female members had finally begun to ease. His father, the Alpha at the time, hadn't recovered and Adam feared he never would. Christian had always been a wonderful father and leader, but Adam had had to step into the position.

Adam was terrified.

Since it wasn't a full moon, Adam didn't have anyone to currently watch over, but he still felt the pressure of knowing every member of the Pack was relying on him in one way or another. He'd barely turned twenty-eight and already he was responsible for so much.

There didn't seem to be any break coming soon. He had some hard decisions to make, the first being a Pack Beta or Enforcer. Every Pack had a second in command. Whether they chose a Beta who would be the liaison between Pack member and Alpha, or an Enforcer who played a more hands-on role as protector remained up to each Alpha. Christian had led with a Beta, but as the man wanted to ready to retire, Adam would need to make up his own mind.

No one knew yet but Adam was leaning more toward having an Enforcer. His best friend, Cain, served as Enforcer for one of the largest Packs and Adam liked the confidence that Pack had in the inner circle. After the attack on Mindy, there had been no question that his Pack needed to feel safe again. Adam truly believed that an Enforcer would benefit them the most.

Adam wanted to have an open door to his Pack. They weren't even a third of the size of Cain's, but the protection of every member would be his top priority. It was going to be hard to tell his father, though. Christian barely came out of his room and only spoke to a few people.

Luckily Christian's oldest friend, Logan, was visiting for a while. Logan currently served as the Beta for the largest Pack in Texas so it was pretty special that Logan and Gage, the Alpha, were giving Logan time to help Christian.

Hopefully there could be help for his father.

Every night when Adam laid down his head, he worried his father would decide to end his existence. It was that fear that kept him from turning to his dad when he needed him the most. He could call Cain, but his best friend was trying to sort out a new relationship and Adam didn't want to bother him. That left him on his own to figure out things. The only other people he stayed close to were Pack. That wasn't to say he wasn't getting assistance from other Alphas or the Council. Adam spent more time on the phone than he'd ever thought he would. Most people had advice or recommendations, but the choice fell to him.

From high on a ridge, he could see the entire expanse of his territory and it filled him. Yes, becoming the Alphas was full of complications, but he wouldn't want anyone else to take over.

The land, people and trouble belonged to him.

He threw back his head and howled. Calling out to his Pack that he stood there watching over them. They were safe.

A few of his Pack must have been in their wolf form as well, since he was greeted by answering cries.

Adam took a step and slowly started his way back home. The ridge led him into the small forest that they sped through as a Pack on full-moon runs.

Contrary to popular beliefs, they weren't werewolves. They also didn't have to transform during the full moon. Shifters, they could call on the change whenever they wanted. But Adam still loved to run through the woods with the Pack. It was tradition, not a need. He felt the importance of keeping the familiar customs and rituals.

It was cooler under the canopy of the trees, but Adam didn't mind. He'd raced through earlier, tiring himself out so he'd be able to sleep better when he went to bed. The late nights and early mornings were made more difficult because he couldn't sleep.

As he trotted along, he made sure to keep his senses open. The guards were on duty, stationed all around, but Adam knew they couldn't have too many out watching. Until Adam was sure that every member of his Pack was safe, he would continue to double the protection around his territory.

He didn't come across anyone while making his way to the tree where he'd stashed his clothes.

In the old days, he would have walked naked through the house, up to his room, but as the Alpha, he was trying to learn that he wasn't just another Pack member anymore.

His belongings were right where he'd left them and Adam quickly pulled on his faded jeans and T-shirt before picking up his phone. Four missed calls.

Jeez, he'd only been gone an hour.

Adam listened to the voicemails as he headed up the hill to the back door of the Alpha house. His house now.

When he'd turned twenty-one, Adam had moved into a cabin in the territory, but he now lived back in his old room. He loved the space, set up like a small apartment, but it also meant he was constantly surrounded by people.

Nothing too pressing in the calls. One of the members needed to speak to him, his sister was checking in and there were two calls from friends asking when they'd see him. Adam snorted. *Not for a while.* Since they were humans, he couldn't actually tell them what was going on, so he'd used the excuse his dad was sick. Which wasn't a total lie.

Opening the sliding glass door to enter the house, Adam took a deep breath. He smiled at the smell of cakes and cookies. His sister was getting a head-start on the baking for the next day. She always cooked enough food for an army, and his mouth watered in anticipation. If he didn't have the self-control he did, Adam would weigh five hundred pounds. Laura was truly talented in the kitchen. She'd never left the main house, instead staying with their father and now him. Adam hoped she'd meet someone to mate with one day, but he enjoyed having her close.

He took another breath and found the man he was searching for. His father and former Pack Alpha was in his room. Adam wasn't surprised. Hopefully Christian remained in his human form, because the amount of time his father stayed shifted was really worrying him. Adam had tried to talk to his dad, but Christian still carried around so much guilt. Mindy hadn't been the only female hurt in the recent attacks. She had been just the only one from their Pack.

The only person who seemed to be able reach Christian at all was Logan. Adam selfishly hoped Logan wouldn't have to hurry home to his own Alpha any time soon.

Adam thought about stopping by the kitchen to see Laura, but he knew someone was waiting to talk to him, so headed to his office instead.

Opening the door to the Alpha's workplace, Adam then stepped inside and flipped on the light. He had taken his new position only two months before and hadn't changed anything in the office or the house. He didn't know if he even wanted to, though several friends had suggested it would help the transition if he properly claimed the space and made it his own.

Sometimes, Adam still felt as if he were playing dress-up and his father would walk back into the office and demand Adam stop messing around. Intellectually, he knew that wouldn't happen, but he struggled with it daily. The Council, made up of former Alphas who policed the Packs, had given their blessing for him to take over. His Alpha position was official.

While Adam was growing up, his father had always been there for him and had made running the Pack look so easy. Adam had found out there was a lot that went on behind the scenes he'd never known about.

He needed help, and now that he'd decided on an Enforcer instead of a Beta, he needed to figure out who would be best for the role. There wasn't anyone in the Pack he thought fit the bill for what he needed. He would have to bring someone in, which wouldn't be easy. Of course, first he needed to find the man or woman.

Once he'd reached the desk, he turned on the computer and waited for it to boot up. As he did so, he fired off a text to the sentry on duty inside to send in the Pack member who needed to speak to him.

He called out for them to enter when the knock came, but it wasn't until he saw the young woman peek around the male shifter that Adam cursed not having gone to his room and changing first. He was tired and had just wanted to find out how he could help. Of course, the minute he hadn't follow proper procedure, Tasha Johnson would show up.

Adam had been lusting after Tasha for over a year now. The young woman didn't seem to notice him, though. She was raising her teenage sister single-handedly, and as much as the Pack helped, Tasha seemed to prefer to do most things on her own. Which meant she worked a lot and didn't hang around the same party crowd Adam did.

Things were changing, though, so maybe he'd be able to prove to her she could put her trust in him. Not only as an Alpha, but perhaps more. He adjusted his hard-on under the desk before he stood and smiled at her.

Tasha Johnson had followed the guard inside the Alpha house and down the hall. When they'd reached a large oak door, she'd run her sweaty palms over her jeans, as her escort had knocked. She hated to bring her family problems to the new Alpha, but she didn't know where else to turn.

The low voice that had told them to enter sent a shiver down her spine. As the guard had opened the door, then moved out of the way, she'd peeked inside and gotten a good look at the new Pack leader. She'd stayed back at the entrance as Bryan had gone and spoke to the Alpha.

She'd known Adam for years, even though they'd never been close, and had admired him from a distance for a long time now. The fact that she was about to face him alone made her stomach flutter with nerves. He was just so good-looking and she did not want to make a fool of herself in front of him. Plus, she really did need his help.

He'd smiled and liquid arousal had pooled inside her panties. She'd shifted to relieve the pressure, certain if she didn't calm her body, he would be able to tell. A shifter's sense of smell was strong and, as the Alpha bonded more with the Pack, there would be no hiding anything from him.

Her attraction to the Alpha wasn't something she should be worried about, but she couldn't help it. In addition, she really needed to keep her mind off why she was even there. Even just for a minute. She was on the verge of freaking out.

Her entire life had been about showing her younger sister love and acceptance. Just when Tasha had begun to believe she'd done a good job raising the teen, Crystal had taken off. Now Tasha had to go to the one man she tried to avoid.

When Adam stood and motioned her in, she didn't miss the large bulge trapped in his jeans. The sight of his package did nothing to tame her own desire. Oh, the man just oozed raw sexuality.

The guard left the office without another word and closed the door behind him. The Alpha's scent surrounded her and Tasha struggled not to close her eyes and breathe deeply. She had serious business to discuss.

"Bryan told me that you had a family emergency and needed my help," Adam said as he gestured for her to sit.

Weak-kneed, Tasha gladly took a seat on the worn brown leather couch and clasped her hands in her lap. She should be concentrating on getting her sister back instead of on her desire for a male. Maybe she was a terrible sister, like Crystal had accused her of being. Tears pooled in her eyes, but she refused to let them fall. Even if she were the worst parent figure, Crystal's safety was her first priority. "Yes, Alpha. I need to talk you about my sister, Crystal." *Keep it formal, don't think of him as the man I've been dreaming about. Should be easy enough.*

He sat in the chair across from her and leaned forward. "I'm listening. Whatever you need, I'll help. But call me Adam. There's no need to be so formal."

Well, there goes that plan. Crystal, think about Crystal. Where should I start? "I'm not sure if your father told you about my family when you took over the Pack." She was so nervous she could feel sweat bead on her forehead. She hated talking about her family and sharing the pain of her past.

She saw the sympathy in his eyes when he spoke. "Why don't you tell me?"

Tasha took a deep breath before starting, "Five years ago, my father left our family. I'm still not sure where he went, but my mother didn't take it well. Six months after he left, she ended her existence and left Crystal with me. She was eleven."

He nodded but didn't comment. She appreciated him letting her get the story out quickly. The sooner she finished, the sooner she could once again bury her pain.

"I've tried to do the best I can, but I don't always understand what she is going through. My sister Crystal is a...non-shifter." Tasha waited for his reaction. Being a non-shifter was an embarrassment for her sister. Tasha only saw how wonderful her sibling was instead of whether she could shift or not, and even though she didn't fully understand the issue, she always respected Crystal's wishes. They hadn't told many people, because a lot of Pack members considered non-shifters lower class.

"Go on," he told her gently, and she didn't hear or see anything negative from him.

"Crystal's had a hard time lately with some of the kids from school. That's why I think she ran away." That and she claimed Tasha was trying to keep her away from humans but insisted the both of them attend Pack activities. But Tasha didn't want to get into that right now. She'd only been trying to show Crystal that everyone accepted her, loved her.

"Do you have any idea where she could have gone?" he asked and Tasha just stared at him. Didn't he want to ask questions about the non-shifter part of the story? He didn't say anything more, instead simply waited for her reply.

"I do. I talked to her best friend and she told me that Crystal has been talking to a boy in the city over the Internet. She probably went there." Tasha spoke quickly. "I have his name and number. I keep calling, but no one is answering. He is older and I'm worried about what he might do to her."

Adam leaned over and placed his hand over hers. "Give me the details and I will find her. I promise you that."

Tasha could feel tears threaten to fall in relief. "Thank you, Adam. Thank you."

He squeezed her hand before releasing it. "That is what I am here for. Do you have the information with you?"

Tasha nodded and dug in her purse for her small notebook. Her hand still tingled from where Adam had touched her. "I wrote it all down." She tore out a page and handed it to him, hoping he didn't notice her hands shaking.

"I'll work on this and keep you in the loop on what I find out," he told her as he stood. "I know realize it's useless to tell you not to worry, but I hope you know you can trust me."

"I do," she assured him. She wasn't lying. Even if Adam hadn't been the Alpha, there was a good chance Christian would have charged his son to handle this, anyway. She wasn't sure who Adam would send, but she understood knew he would keep his word about finding Crystal.

"I'm glad," Adam said. "Why don't you head home in case she calls? Let me know if you hear from her."

She nodded as he held out his hand and helped her to her feet.

An electric current ran between them and she gasped in surprise. Adam seemed stunned for an instant before he grinned at her. That wicked look on his face had Tasha longing to reach out and grab hold of him.

It wasn't just the fact she found him attractive, making her want the strength of his arms around her. She was tired and heartbroken. It was hard raising a teenager, even with help from her friends and adopted family. That was what the Pack meant to her. Honorary aunts, uncles, cousins and more.

"Hey, it's okay," Adam said, pulling her close.

Tasha allowed him to comfort her and it felt so right. He wrapped his strong arms around her shoulders and she buried her face in his chest. This time, she couldn't hold the tears at bay. She sobbed into his shirt and let go of all her worry.

He rubbed her back and murmured, "It's okay. We'll find her. I did some pretty shitty things when I was her age. You raised her well and she knows right from wrong."

Oh, God! She had needed to hear the words.

Once she felt as though she had control again, she patted his chest before pulling away. The expression on his face was so soft and caring she almost started crying again. How had the two of them fought this connection that was so obvious?

"I'll walk you out," Adam told her as he stepped away.

"Okay," she agreed.

He placed his hand on her lower back and she jolted. Yes, the attraction was there and strong. They didn't speak as they left the office and strolled down the hall toward the front door. Tasha noticed that nothing had been changed inside the Alpha house and she was surprised. It was quite normal for a new Alpha to at least make small modifications so the Pack accepted the transition of power. It had only been a couple of months since Christian had stepped down, but Adam needed to take control.

Not that Tasha felt she should voice her thoughts just yet. There was always more than what appeared on the surface when it came to Alphas, and if the dark circles under Adam's beautiful eyes were any indication, this new Alpha was struggled with something.

She hated to add to his stress, but some things couldn't be helped. It did comfort her that even if he were going through his own troubles, he was willing to give his time and attention to her needs.

She had no doubt that Adam would make a wonderful Alpha.

He opened the front door for her and she paused to look up at him. "I know that you have other things to worry about—"

"No," he interrupted. "You don't need to concern yourself about that. We concentrate on your sister."

Tasha reached down and gripped his hand. She didn't need to say anything else. Her touch showed her appreciation and since she was barely hanging on to her emotions, it would be best to remain silent.

She released him before walking out of the door then jogging down the stairs. Her old car sat in front of the large Alpha house, standing out as a reminder that she didn't fit in there. She wasn't fancy or knock-out gorgeous. She was kind of plain and men didn't usually pay her too much attention. But she felt his.

The entire time she moved away from him, she could sense his gaze on her. It felt good to hold the interest of such a gorgeous and powerful shifter. If she put a little more wiggle in her hips, who could blame her?

It wasn't until she climbed behind the wheel that she glanced up toward the house. Adam was still there, leaning against the door frame, and his hot gaze bore into her. She shivered. Maybe she would have something to thank her sister for once she'd dragged her hormonal teenage butt back.

Tasha pushed the key in the ignition, then started her car. She'd given the information she had to the Alpha, but that didn't mean that she was going to lay it all at his feet. If she didn't hear from Crystal tonight, she would head into the city herself.

Adam waited until the brake lights on Tasha's car were out of sight before he closed the front door. A missing teenager was not what the Pack needed. Not only was there a chance of the young girl getting really hurt but she belonged to his Pack and he'd vowed to keep them safe.

He turned toward his office to begin researching the name and number that Tasha had provided. She hadn't told him how old the guy who Crystal had been talking to was and Adam wanted as much information as possible.

Halfway to his workspace, he spotted the figure leaning against the wall. Adam frowned and hurried his pace.

"Is my dad okay?" he asked Logan.

"He's fine," Logan assured him. He grinned before clasping Adam on the shoulder. "I did want to talk to you if you have a minute."

"Sure." Adam waved Logan toward his office.

"Everything okay?" Logan asked, walking in front of him.

Adam followed and closed the door behind them. He didn't want anyone else to hear about Pack business. He trusted and respected Logan.

Logan and Christian had been friends Adam's entire life, so even though they'd lived in different Packs, Logan had always been around. He was like an uncle to Adam.

"One of our teenagers took off to the city to meet up with an older boy," Adam told him.

Logan chuckled. "Sometimes I don't know how we make it from about fifteen to nineteen."

Adam nodded his agreement as he headed toward the

small bar in the corner of the room. "Drink?"

"Whatever you're having is fine," Logan said.

"Whiskey?" Adam offered.

"Yeah," Logan answered. Instead of sitting, he prowled around while Adam fixed the drinks. Logan might seem fine, but it was obvious to Adam something was on the older shifter's mind.

Adam finished pouring the liquor, then picked up both glasses. He handed one to Logan. "What's up?" He couldn't help but be worried about his dad.

"Let's sit," Logan suggested.

That couldn't be good, but Adam walked toward the couch and sat. Logan joined him. As much as Adam wanted to press Logan, he waited. Finally, after Logan had taken a sip, he sighed before setting his drink on the table.

"I have to return home," Logan informed him.

Damn, it wasn't half an hour ago that Adam had been hoping Logan would be able to stay a while. "Right away?" Adam asked.

Logan rubbed his hands roughly over his face. "Yeah, my Alpha's mate is pregnant and he's given me as much time as he can, but he needs me back. Gage is worried about security while she's expecting. I have to return to my job."

"I know," Adam said. It hurt, but Logan had already spent so much time with his dad. "I'm just worried about my father."

"He's doing much better," Logan said.

"I don't know," Adam confessed. "He barely talks to me anymore."

"Give him time," Logan said. "He's working through some issues and it's taking him time to get his head on straight. He will, though. He loves you and your sister."

Adam sighed. He appreciated Logan's words, but that didn't mean he could or would stop worrying. "I wish you didn't have to leave."

"That's what I wanted to discuss," Logan said.

Adam snapped his head over to look at him.

"I'd like to ask Christian to come back home with me. It will give him a chance to get away from everything and hopefully settle."

He wanted to say no, scream it, even, but Adam knew Logan was probably right. His dad was going to waste away in his room if he didn't get a change of scenery. Adam was hurt, but Logan was dead-on.

Adam rose and paced to the opposite side of the room. The blinds were open and he could see the backyard. The pool, barbecue and lawn chairs. They'd used to sit out there at night, he and his dad, never talking about much. Just enjoying each other's company and the night coming alive around them. He missed those times. If he didn't give his dad space to heal, he might not ever get back the most important man to him.

"Take him with you," Adam said without turning around.

He didn't hear Logan rise, but he wasn't surprised when a hand clamped down on his shoulder.

"I'll take good care of him," Logan promised.

Adam nodded.

"Can I make another suggestion?" Logan asked quietly.

He turned, smiling. "Sure."

"Maybe it would be a good idea for you to have a break of your own," Logan said.

"I can't just leave," Adam said.

"Your dad left the territory. Went on vacation or visited other Alphas," Logan pointed out.

"He had his inner circle in place," Adam said.

"And until you choose your own, they're still here," Logan pointed out. "Let them help. Yes, most have been in the position so long they're ready to retire, but no one is abandoning you."

"I feel alone," Adam confessed.

"I know," Logan said. "It's one of the things your dad and I argue about. He's proud of you. Damn, boy, your father believes in you. He doesn't see that you still need some guidance."

"What should I do?" Adam asked. It was the first time he'd asked anyone that question.

"Go bring your teenage Pack member back," Logan said. "That will help you see what you're fighting for. Connect you to the Pack."

It wasn't a terrible idea. If he left early enough, he might only be gone a day or two. He could rely on his dad's men. Plus, his sister was there, along with the guards. "I might just do that."

"Good." Logan pulled him into a quick hug, then slapped his back. "Good."

As Logan let go of him to head for the exit, Adam was so damn grateful. "Hey, Logan," he called.

Logan turned at the door.

"Thank you."

"Of course." Logan smiled. "You can call me anytime. I'm here for you, too."

Adam let the older shifter go. It was time he made some calls so he could take care of Pack business. In addition, he'd be able to drop in and see Cain. Cain's mate was finishing school and he was currently staying in an apartment not far from the campus.

With a plan forming, Adam headed to his desk to get the ball rolling.

Chapter Two

It was still dark when Adam closed the door to the house and walked to his SUV. The early morning had a bite to it, but it was supposed to turn into a beautiful afternoon. He hoped that he could make the day better by bringing home a lost teenager. Logan had been right last night. Adam needed to go out and get hands-on. Plus, a small break might help him clear his head.

He'd made two important calls the night before. The first had been to his best friend. Cain had jumped at the chance to help. It seemed his friend was missing excitement, as well. Cain had opened a training center in the city for his guards and potential guards and while this kept him busy, Cain had complained he wanted to investigate something. Adam requesting his help had Cain almost giddy. Emily had even gotten on the phone and thanked Adam. It turned out Cain being so restless was driving her crazy. Adam would spend the night with his old friend as he searched for Crystal.

Cain had even pressed Adam about the decisions that he needed to make and Adam realized Cain had been worried about him. And that made Adam feel like shit. Sure, he hadn't wanted to bother Cain, but now Cain felt as if he'd done something wrong. Adam had some reassuring to do.

The second call he'd made had been to Gage Wolf, Logan's Alpha, to thank him. Gage had assured Adam that Christian would be safe and cared after while he was with them. Adam had believed him.

Gage had surprised Adam by asking him to bring Crystal by his house once she was home again.

Marissa, Gage's mate, was also a non-shifter and had set up some chat rooms and communication for other non-shifters. Gage had believed Crystal would benefit from the visit, so Adam had quickly agreed.

After he'd finished his calls, he'd sat back in his chair, realizing he'd been an idiot.

Adam had the best Alphas in the country around him, ones he called friends, and he wasn't utilizing their expertise. He'd been doing his Pack a disservice by not calling on his contacts. Adam had been worried he'd be judged an unworthy Alpha. That couldn't be further from the truth.

He'd slept better the night before than he had in months. For the first time in what seemed like forever, he'd woken refreshed and with a positive attitude. Adam threw his overnight bag into the vehicle, turned around and ran right into Tasha.

He reached out and steadied her as she almost fell. The electricity that sparked between them was the same as it had been the night before. It was an interesting development. "What are you doing here?" he asked, his hands still clasped around her upper arms.

Her eyes were wide, but her smile was bright. "I want to come with you," she told him and lifted a backpack to show him.

Adam looked from the backpack to the woman several times. He really shouldn't be surprised. Everything he'd seen and learned about Tasha had shown she was very involved when it came to her sister. He just didn't know how he would concentrate on finding Crystal and making the decisions he needed with Tasha with him. Fuck, he ached for her. Pursuing her wouldn't be proper as he was now the Alpha and Adam wished he'd tried to get to know her better earlier. "How'd you even know I would be going?"

She rolled her eyes but finally answered. "I guessed. Well, I guessed someone would and I want to help find my sister."

"I don't think it's a good idea," Adam said. "You need to be here if she comes home. Plus, it could be dangerous." Adam meant every word he said but left out the part where it would be easier for him as well.

"She's an angry and scared teenage girl. You might be her Alpha, but she doesn't really know you," Tasha said. "What are you going to do if she refuses to come with you? Throw her over your shoulder and carry her to the car? That won't look suspicious."

She was right. If Crystal was feeling confused enough to travel and stay with a man she didn't know, Adam being her Alpha wasn't going to matter much. If he took Tasha with him, at least she would be there to help him handle the teenager. He studied her, wondering how long they would keep playing with fire. Sooner or later, one of them was going to ignite. The attraction between them was burning. He sighed, knowing he didn't have any other choice. Plus, he could take the opportunity to talk to her about taking Crystal to see Marissa.

He picked up the bag she'd dropped. "Get in the car." Adam hoped he didn't regret his choice. He would still need to use the time to think about the Pack. An interesting email had come in the night before that had offered a solution. Adam knew if he went with his gut and decided to go in the direction he was leaning, a lot of people wouldn't be happy. Cain being one of them. But Adam had to do what was best for *his* Pack. He'd already decided to speak with Gage about his options. Hopefully Gage would be able to remain unbiased, unlike Cain. There were just some things that Cain was too stubborn to even consider. "We need to leave," he told Tasha, shaking away his thoughts. It was time to get on the road. He had leisure on the long drive to go over his options.

Tasha didn't gloat. Rather, she just nodded, turned and opened the passenger door. He appreciated that. He could also use the hours they'd be stuck together in the vehicle to learn more about the intriguing woman. It would be a form of torture, knowing he couldn't have her, but Adam still wanted to know every detail of Tasha's life.

He tossed Tasha's bag next to his, then slammed the hatch closed before taking a deep breath of his territory, using the scent to calm him. He'd be home soon and hopefully have a better idea of how to lead.

* * * *

"Tasha?"

Tasha snapped her head around and he realized she had drifted off. He hated to wake her, but they'd reached their first destination. He grinned at her as she blinked sleepily at him. They'd talked for the first hour about the Pack, her job, Crystal, common friends, and it had been nice. The easy banter between them had been lively and fun. Tasha was quick-witted and hilarious. She was also adorable, especially as she blushed.

"I can't believe I fell asleep," she said.

He chuckled. It hadn't been a problem for him. Adam had enjoyed sneaking peeks at her. Even more when her shirt had risen to show her flat, tan stomach. He'd itched to put his hands on her but had resisted. She might have been receptive, but he had to remember his place.

Tasha didn't seem to be on the same page, though. She leaned toward him and poked his arm. "Are you laughing at me?"

"Of course not," he lied.

She harrumphed at him. "Don't forget, Alpha, I can find out where you sleep at night."

That sounded too good to him. "Oh, yeah?" he taunted.

"Yep," she said. "I'll post a video of you snoring and drooling."

He laughed loudly. She was delightful. "How do you know I snore and drool?"

Tasha narrowed her eyes. "You seem the type."

He'd give anything to show her how wrong she was. He'd

never been accused of snoring and wasn't too worried that he drooled, either. "You have an evil streak in you."

The grin that spread across her face was wicked. "You have no idea."

They both jumped when a loud knock came on the passenger window. Adam had been so lost in Tasha that he hadn't been paying attention to his surroundings. That could be dangerous and was another reason he needed to steer clear of his feelings for Tasha.

"What the hell?" Tasha muttered.

Adam groaned and unbuckled his seatbelt. "That's my friend, Cain." Cain grinned at them as he leaned to peer inside the vehicle. Adam knew his friend would be teasing him later. At least Cain would behave in front of Tasha. Well, Adam hoped he would. Sometimes he couldn't be sure what Cain was going to do. "We'd better get out before he decides to join us in here."

Tasha unbuckled her seatbelt as Adam did the same before they exited the SUV. Cain held open Tasha's door and it was obvious that he was picking up on the attraction between them. Yep, Cain smiled wide and winked at him before he held out his hand to Tasha.

"Hey, there," Cain said. "I wasn't aware Adam was bringing anyone with him. He's been holding out on me."

Tasha shook his hand, then shrugged. "He didn't know. I sort of pressured him into letting me tag along."

Cain laughed. "I'm sure you had to twist him arm."

"Cain," Adam growled in warning.

"What?" Cain blinked innocently at him, but Adam wasn't buying it. Tasha obviously agreed, since she looked over her shoulder at him and shrugged again.

"Just ignore him," Adam told her. "He's barely house-trained."

"Ha!" Cain pointed at him. "I'm going to tell Emily you said that. My mate's going to hurt you, again."

Adam glared at Cain, but his friend only continued to bounce on the balls of his feet and grin. Adam had unwisely offered to teach Cain's mate some self-defense after the attacks a couple of months ago. Adam should have been worried when Cain had been a little too excited. It turned out that Emily had been training with Cain since she'd been a young girl and she could take down both male and female shifters without any problems. Adam had ended up flat on the mat several times before he realized he'd been played.

"I have no idea why I'm friends with you," Adam complained.

"Because I bring excitement to your life," Cain replied easily.

"Here," Adam said as he came around the vehicle. "Let me introduce you to more civilized people. Cain, get our bags."

"Yes, your majesty," Cain said with a bow.

Adam ignored him, again. He could see Emily and Tony, Cain's older brother, waiting at the front of the apartment building so he placed his hand on the small of Tasha's back and led her forward.

He greeted Emily with a kiss on her cheek and shook hands with Tony. While Adam wasn't as close to him as he was to Cain, he had a lot of respect for Tony — everyone did. They both greeted Tasha warmly and he was pleased that neither was in the same playful mood as Cain. They could both be just as bad. Must be something in that Pack's water.

"Glad you could make it," Emily told him. "Cain's missed you."

He nodded in acceptance. He still felt bad that he hadn't been confiding in his best friend. He turned to Cain's brother. "I didn't know you were in town," he said. "It's good to see you."

Tony clapped a hand on Adam's back, then turned to lead the way inside as he answered. "Had a meeting earlier with the Alpha Council and our friendly government officials."

Well, that explained it. Recently, the Council had decided to come out of hiding and let the public know that shifters really did exist. The government was helping the paranormals come out to the world and it so happened that there were some powerful shifters in place already. Adam wasn't sure what he thought about the news. To him, it couldn't have come at a worse time. While he'd love to stop hiding his true self, he also worried how humans would react to knowing that shifters were all around them. Scared people could end up being dangerous.

"The government?" Tasha asked.

Tony glanced back over his shoulder at Tasha before darting a look at him. Adam hadn't revealed to his Pack what was going on yet.

One of the reasons he was so concerned about getting his inner circle in place was because of the chance of the Pack being exposed. It wasn't a worry he wanted others to have to deal with so soon.

Tasha hadn't missed the look from Tony.

"You don't have to tell me," she assured them.

That helped Adam make up his mind and he nodded his approval of telling her. This might be a chance for him to see how a member of his Pack would feel about the situation. Tasha was a smart girl and he was curious how she'd react.

The elevator doors opened and they stepped inside. "The Council is considering making the shifter population public to the world. They want to come out of hiding."

Tasha gasped. "You're kidding!"

"No," Adam said. "They are very serious and have actually been thinking about this for years. It was just recently that they asked each Alpha for their opinions."

"What did you say?" Tasha asked.

Adam couldn't tell what she thought, other than being shocked. "I haven't said anything. It's still not one-hundred percent certain and I need time to think about it."

Tasha nodded. "Makes sense." She turned to Tony. "Do you suppose we'll actually do it?"

"Probably," Tony answered. "A lot of accidental deaths could be avoided when we're in our shifter form if we could come out."

"Tony here will be the face of the Packs. When it comes out to the public that shifters exist, he'll stand in front of the world and let them see we're as normal as them," Cain said.

The elevator dinged before the doors opened. Adam motioned the others out ahead of him.

"Normal?" Adam teased. "I don't know anyone that's normal." He didn't want Tasha to start worrying about what might or might not happen so he tried to ease them out of the conversation.

Emily and Tasha laughed while Cain reached out and smacked his shoulder.

Adam grinned up at his friend. Damn, he'd really missed screwing around with Cain and not having so many responsibilities. Speaking of, he needed to get them back on track. "Did you get any more information for me?" he asked Cain.

"Sure did," Cain said as they walked down a small hallway to an open door. "Let's go in and sit."

Adam hoped that Cain wasn't going to give them bad news. He placed his hand on the small of Tasha's back again, this time for support.

The apartment they were led into was big and cluttered, although clean. Right away he felt comfortable. Adam knew it wasn't the place that Emily had rented on her own. Instead, when Cain had moved to the city to be with her, they had leased this space together. They had a house back home with the Pack so this was just a temporary residence. Still, he liked the way it reflected both Cain and Emily.

Adam sat on the plush couch, pleased when Tasha dropped down close to him. Tony sat in one of the chairs across from them and Cain took the other. Emily settled next to her mate on the arm of the seat.

"No one was at the apartment last night when I went by," Cain told the group. "But when I talked to some of the neighbors, they gave me the names of a couple of clubs he likes to frequent."

"Crystal's too young to get into any of the clubs here,"

Tasha argued.

"I have a feeling the places this guy goes to aren't that interested in checking IDs," Cain told her. "I also asked Tony to dig a little deeper for us."

Tony cleared his throat. "Mike Lawson has a minor criminal background. Mostly petty theft and some drug charges, but it was enough to reinforce that we need to get Crystal back as soon as possible."

"This isn't good." Tasha dropped her head.

"There wasn't anything domestic or against women, so I think she's safe there, but I'd hate to see her get mixed up with the drug crowd," Tony said.

"I want to say that she'd never touch drugs, but I never thought she'd run away, either," Tasha confessed.

Adam reached over and held her hand. "We'll find her."

Tasha nodded. "We have to."

"One of the bars opens early," Cain said. "We should get changed and see if we find her there. If not, we'll hit some of the other places before circling back around."

"Changed?" Adam asked. He didn't think Cain was suggesting they shift and run around in the city.

Cain grinned. "We're going clubbing, baby. We need to blend in so no one asks too many questions. We don't want Mike tipped off we're looking for him."

Adam glanced at Tasha.

"It makes sense," Tasha said. "But I didn't bring any clothes that would really fit in with going to bars."

Emily jumped up. "You look about the same size as me. I'll loan you some and we'll get ready while the guys catch up."

Cain rose, as well. "You're not going," he said to his mate.

Emily had already taken a few steps away from him, but at his words she whirled on Cain. "I'm sorry, what?"

Adam placed his hand on Tasha's knee to keep her in place. He could see the upcoming conversation turning ugly really quickly.

"You're not going," Cain repeated.

"Yes, I am," Emily snapped right back. "We're looking for a teenage girl and I want to help."

"No." Cain crossed his arms over his chest.

Tony leaned back in his chair and glanced over at Adam, shaking his head. They both knew that Cain was too overprotective of Emily and that she often rebelled.

"Who's going to stop me?" she taunted. "You?"

"You know damn well I will," Cain said.

"You'll try," Emily said. "But as the man I love, you'll always realize that if you do, you're going to be sleeping on the couch for several days."

"Whatever," Cain scoffed.

Shit, Adam couldn't believe Cain was being so dumb. They all knew that Emily could take care of herself and he was just being pigheaded.

Emily fisted her hand on her hips. "Excuse me? I know I didn't hear you right."

"You are not going out, to a bar, with people who very well could be criminals," Cain stated firmly.

"Because I might get hurt?" she mocked. "The little woman should stay home, barefoot, making your dinner?"

"You know damn well that's not what I mean." Cain threw up his hands in frustration.

"And you know that it would be helpful having me come along," Emily argued. "I can also take care of myself. You taught me that, as well."

Cain deflated. "Nothing can ever happen to you. Ever. I love you too much and it would destroy me."

"I know." Emily shuffled toward her mate. "I love you, too. But you can't keep me locked up in a tower because you're worried. I still have to live my life and if I can help, I'm going to."

"Fine." Cain wrapped his arm around her waist. "But if anyone touches even one hair on your head, I will rip their throat out."

She nodded before kissing him long and deeply.

Tasha squirmed in her seat as Cain immediately yanked

Emily closer and the kiss turned dirty and hot. Adam looked away from the couple. He was embarrassed to be watching, but he was also jealous.

Cain and Emily belonged together. It was as obvious to him as anything else in the world. He wanted that kind of love and devotion. He just didn't think it was possible.

He glanced over at Tasha and found her gaze on him. He bet she would be a great kisser.

"Okay," Tony said loudly. "We don't really need a show."

Cain groaned but pulled back. Emily glanced around as though she'd forgotten they were even in the room. She blushed prettily.

"Yes, well," Emily smoothed down her shirt before turning to Crystal. "Shall we?"

Adam waited until the ladies had left the room before he winked at Tony and turned on his friend. "I have to say I never thought I'd see you like this," Adam teased with a grin.

Cain sat back down and crossed his big arms over his chest. "What's that supposed to mean?"

Adam held up his hands in a mock surrender. "Nothing, man, you just seem to be so...so..." He struggled for the right word.

"Whipped!" Tony added when Adam trailed off.

Cain's eyes narrowed and Adam leaned back to get out of the line of fire. Then the big Enforcer surprised him by smiling. "Just wait," he said, still grinning. "Just wait until you meet your mates. I am going to remember every time you teased me and it's going to be ten times worse."

Tony groaned, but Adam looked toward the hallway where the women had disappeared.

He heard Cain and Tony laughing and glanced back at them. "What?"

"Got it bad, man," Cain said.

"No," Adam said. "It's not like that."

"Why not?" Tony asked.

Adam sighed. He really did not want to have this

conversation, but he had known it was coming. Maybe it would be better to just get it out of the way. "She's a member of my Pack."

"And?" Cain pressed.

"It wouldn't be right," Adam said.

Cain shook his head, but it was Tony who drew Adam's attention. Tony leaned forward to brace his elbows on his knees, looking at Adam. "Do you really believe that?" Tony asked. "That you can't date someone from your Pack?"

"I don't know," Adam said with a shrug. "I don't want Tasha or anyone to feel that they have to be with me because I'm their Alpha. It's not right."

"I would normally agree with you," Tony said. "Except for a few important points."

Adam sat up straighter. He was really interested in Tony's perspective.

"You are not the type of man or shifter who'd ever take advantage of someone," Tony said. "You are harder on yourself than anyone else. There is no one who is more honest or thoughtful in your entire Pack. There is a reason you were chosen to lead and it had nothing to do with your father being the previous Alpha."

Adam nodded. He wanted to believe his friends, but it wasn't that easy.

"You also deserve to be happy," Cain added.

Adam glanced at him.

"What?" Cain said defensively. "I notice shit. You are wearing yourself down to the bone, so worried you're going to screw up. If it was up to you, there wouldn't be anyone in your life because you think you need to give the Pack one-hundred percent of your attention."

"I do," Adam replied.

"No," Tony objected. "That will lead you to burning out and eventually resenting your Pack. You need to find a way to balance what's best for them and you."

"And you think the answer is a woman?" Adam said, dismissively.

"No," Cain responded with a growl. "We think the answer is you being happy. Tasha makes you happy. It's obvious to us and we've been with the two of you for less than an hour."

"I think it's pretty fucked up that you think I'm happy when a teenage girl is missing," Adam snapped. He didn't know why he was getting so irritated, but Cain and Tony needed to back off.

Cain chuckled and Adam scowled at him.

"That right there," Cain said as he pointed at Adam, "is a reaction that would have come from me."

"And often did," Tony agreed.

Cain laughed. "And why was I such an asshole?"

"Because you were denying your feelings for Emily," Adam conceded.

"Right," Cain praised. "No one is saying that you are happy that one of your Pack members is missing. What we are telling you is that you are comfortable with Tasha and she makes you smile."

"Which is perfectly okay," Tony said. "Even if she's in your Pack."

Adam sighed. "If I promise to think about what you've said, can you just stop?"

"Yep," Cain agreed, then bounced up. "Now let's go find you some slutty jeans and doll you up."

"Christ," Adam muttered as he followed Cain. He really needed more mature friends. When Cain peered back over his shoulder, Adam just shook his head. Who was Adam kidding? He had the best buds in the entire world. Antics and all. He was a very lucky man.

* * * *

Adam winced as the loud music assaulted his ears. This was the third club they'd visited and he was getting tired of the crowds and music.

There hadn't been a sign of Crystal and he was growing

more and more worried. The group had split up to hit all of the clubs on the list. This was the last one on his and Tasha's. He'd spoken to Cain and Tony and they weren't having any better luck. Cain had assigned one of the guards, who was in the city for training, to accompany Tony so no one was alone. At least there shouldn't be too much trouble if they did come across Mike and his group. Adam wasn't sure what he'd do if Crystal wasn't with the human when someone eventually found him.

Tasha pointed to the back of the club and, with a heavy sigh, he nodded. They circled the room, looking for the teenager. He tried to ignore the looks Tasha was getting from the men around them. The wolf inside him wanted to growl and threaten them, but Adam kept a tight rein on his instincts. He might be fighting his attraction to Tasha, but that didn't give him an excuse to act territorial. She didn't belong to him.

He ignored the small voice in his head that whispered, *yet*.

Whether he wanted to or not, Adam found himself thinking about what Cain and Tony had said earlier. If Tasha was interested in him, then maybe he should see where their attraction led. As long as she knew it was completely her choice, perhaps he had a chance.

When they'd almost reached the back corner, Tasha grabbed his sleeve and tugged.

"She's here!" She pointed to the darker spot.

Adam took in the men who sat, surrounding the girl, at the table. The female had her elbows on the table and looked miserable. His heart sped up as relief washed over him. She appeared uninjured. He glanced at Tasha and saw the same look on her face.

"I can get her out of here, but if they fight me, it can turn ugly." He pulled Tasha close to speak in her ear. He ignored the tingling in his fingertips as he brushed against her bare midriff.

"What do we do?" she asked, leaning in.

A sweet perfume scent wafted up and he grew even harder than he already was. His cock had been half-hard since he'd first seen her in the low-rise jeans and silk tank back at the apartment. Now his cock throbbed, trapped behind the zipper of his own jeans. Adam quickly needed to put some space between him and Tasha.

"I'm going to text Cain and Tony. Let's stay over by the wall and keep an eye on her."

Tasha nodded and moved to the back wall. It would give them a good view of the table but keep them out of Crystal's sight. There were enough patrons that unless Crystal was searching for someone, she shouldn't pick up on their scent.

Tasha walked in front of him as Adam typed a group message. Before he could catch up to her, a man in black leather had boxed her against the wall.

Adam felt a growl start deep in his chest and clenched his fists, trying to control his temper. Pushing through the crowd, he walked up to the two and leaned close to Tasha, pressing his body into hers.

"Hey, baby," he said loud enough for the other man to hear.

Playing along, Tasha rubbed her body against his and ran her hands over his chest. He resisted the urge to drop a kiss onto her plump lips.

"What took you so long?" she said silkily.

Adam brushed his hand over the low-cut top she wore, feeling her hard nipples. Only after he'd made his point did he look over at the other man. "Can I help you?" He made sure his voice held just the right amount of menace and power. He was an Alpha, after all.

The big man shook his head and walked away.

Tasha leaned into Adam and laughed. "I think you scared him."

"Good. Now keep an eye on your sister." Adam nipped her ear and she shivered. They were playing a dangerous game, but he couldn't help himself.

Tasha nodded as Adam moved his body more securely in

front of hers, giving her just enough room to turn her head and watch the teenager. They did need to blend in and a couple getting friendly was just the right ploy to use. He leaned forward and breathed in her scent.

"Adam," Tasha whispered.

"What is it, honey?" he murmured. Luckily, they didn't have any trouble hearing each other with their enhanced senses. Even with the loud music, Adam could pick up the desire in her voice. The decision was being made for him. Tasha needed him and he wasn't going to fight it.

"I want to feel your lips on me," she said.

Adam had to hold perfectly still so he didn't begin to thrust his hips. That might be taking things further than she wanted. Instead of kissing her as he craved to do, he sucked her earlobe into his mouth. She moaned while slipping her hands around his back to grab his ass.

"Your skin's so soft. I'd like to mark with my mouth, with my hands, my body," he whispered. "As soon as we get your sister to safety, I'm going to do all that and more."

"Promise," she demanded. "Promise me that you aren't just toying with me."

Adam grabbed her chin to make her look him in the eye. "I swear."

She nodded while biting her lip.

"Now watch your sister," he said. "No matter what I do."

He was testing her, both of them, but it was a good reminder that they didn't have privacy so he couldn't be buried inside her balls-deep as he wished.

Adam ran his tongue over the shell of her ear while sliding his hand along her side. Her breathing quickened and he grinned against her neck.

Tasha obviously wasn't going to be shown up, because she moved her hand around until she cupped his erection. "What about you?" she teased before squeezing him. "Can you keep an eye out for your friends while I'm doing this?"

Adam thrust into her hand and latched his mouth on to the side of her neck. His cock was hard enough to pound nails. This had escalated rather quickly and unexpectedly. Knowing that if she continued to touch him he would lose it, Adam captured Tasha's wrists and moved them up over her head. She moaned again, arching her body toward him.

"You promised you wouldn't stop," she complained.

"I'm not," he said. "But I also can't fuck you against this wall."

"But you will later?" she asked.

Adam pulled back enough to peer down at her. "I want to."

Tasha nibbled on her bottom lip.

"What is it?"

"There's times that I think you want me just as much as I do you," she said. "But it's as if you turn it off or something. You confuse you."

Shit! He hadn't meant to send out mixed signals. "I do want you. More than you could ever know."

"So why...?"

"I'm struggling with my attraction to you because I'm your Alpha. I don't want you to think you have to give me what I want just because of my position."

Her laughter surprised him.

Adam began to loosen his hold.

"No," she told him. "Don't stop touching me."

"Okay." He tightened his grip.

"Do I seem like the type of woman who would do anything that I didn't want to?" she asked.

"Well, no," Adam had to admit. Tasha was definitely a woman who knew her own mind. Demanding to come with him to search for her sister had been just one example.

"So, the only thing you have to worry about is keeping your promise to me," Tasha said.

Instead of answering her with words, he licked her neck and thrust his cock against her leg. Now he was going to show her just how much he'd been holding back. She was clutching at his back with one hand while the other was rubbing him hard when a prickle of awareness invaded and told him Cain and Tony had arrived.

Pulling away from Tasha, he grabbed her chin. "We *will* finish this."

Her dark eyes lit up and she licked her lips. "Yes, we will."

Adam adjusted his erection before turning to find his back-up. Catching Cain's gaze, Adam nodded toward the table. Cain and Tony moved from the front door in that direction, and Adam grabbed Tasha's arm, holding her close as they walked to the table.

They all arrived at the same time.

"Tasha!" the young girl greeted, surprised. The rest of the table turned toward them.

"Let's go, Crystal. I'm taking you home," Tasha told her sternly.

Adam didn't miss the look of relief that flashed over the teenager's face as she stood. Before she could move away from the table, Mike grabbed her wrist. Adam recognized him from the picture they'd pulled up off an arrest record.

"We're not done partying, baby. Sit back down." Mike yanked and Crystal fell into his lap.

Adam growled, but before he could react, Tony leaned closer to the table. "Let the girl go." When Mike laughed, Tony glanced over his shoulder. "You see those two men over there?"

Everyone looked, and indeed, there were two large tattooed men only a few feet away.

"Those are the bouncers of this bar. Now, while they won't appreciate you bringing in an underage girl, they probably won't kill you." Tony straightened and raised his voice to make certain everyone around the table could hear the rest. "These two?" He motioned to Adam and Cain. "I can't make that promise."

Cain was scary on his own but with Adam using his Alpha aura as well, the humans didn't stand a chance. The power coming off the two of them had the hair rising on Mike Lawson's arms.

Mike let go of Crystal and she scrambled into Tasha's

hold. Adam nodded to Tony, then wrapped his arms around the females and ushered them out. Crystal was crying in Tasha's arms, sobbing how sorry she was, while Adam held them both tightly. When they hit the fresh air and were away from the crowd, Adam gave the women a little more privacy.

He followed behind at a discreet distance as Tasha murmured to her sister, offering comfort. He hit the Unlock button on the key fob so they could climb in the car's back door. He could still hear Tasha speaking quietly to her sister as he stood by the driver's door. He wouldn't leave until he saw Cain and Tony exit the bar. He didn't know where Emily or Tony's partner was, so he needed to make sure his friends got out okay.

It was less than five minutes before he spotted them. Cain waved Adam off so Adam opened the SUV door to take both his girls away. *His girls.* Adam really liked the sound of that. They were part of his Pack and he had done his job to reunite them. He felt pride in a way that he never had before. Must be the part of his Alpha that was growing the more he bonded with his Pack.

Adam pulled out his cell phone and sent a quick text to Cain, thanking him for the help. He wanted to go ahead and get on the road toward Gage's territory. As much as he missed his best friend, the devastating sobs from the back seat and Crystal's teary explanation about feeling like an outside tore at his heart. He needed to get the young girl to Marissa to have her meet the older non-shifter.

Cain replied quickly that he understood and would be down to see him soon. It was a good thing he and Tasha packed their bags and stashed them in the vehicle. Adam had worried about what condition Crystal was in and hadn't been sure if he would be driving straight back home or not.

He looked in the rearview mirror and caught Tasha's gaze. She smiled at him and he felt lighter already.

Chapter Three

Adam reached over and captured Tasha's hand. She squeezed his palm before rolling her head toward him. They'd already been on the road for over three hours and they were both exhausted.

He'd made a stop earlier at a convenience store where he'd grabbed a large coffee while the women went to the bathroom to change into something more comfortable for the ride home. Apparently, Tasha had packed some of Crystal's favorite lounge pants and T-shirts, which was smart. Adam hadn't even thought about it. They'd left Crystal's backpack back in the city with Mike but Crystal didn't seem too upset about it. He'd also picked up drinks and snacks for them, as well before re-fueling his SUV for the long drive. He'd put a lot of miles in that day and he was ready for a bed, even if it was just turning dark.

Once he had Tasha and Crystal back in the vehicle, it hadn't taken long for the teenager to fall asleep.

"You can close your eyes and rest," Adam told Tasha quietly. He didn't want to wake up Crystal although they weren't too far from Gage's house.

"If I fall asleep, I won't be waking back up. It's okay," she said.

"We only have about thirty more miles if that helps," Adam informed her.

"Should I wake Crystal?" Tasha asked.

"Nah, let her sleep a little longer," Adam suggested. The girl had to be beyond worn out.

"I'm awake," Crystal said as she popped up between their seats.

Adam went to let go of Tasha's hand, unsure if she wanted her sister to know anything about them, but Tasha clung to him.

"Sit back and put your seatbelt on," Tasha ordered.

The teenager sighed heavily before complying. Adam held in his smile. Tasha was such a parent. It was quiet for several minutes before Crystal cleared her throat.

"I'm sorry," she said. "I just wanted to see what it would be like outside the Pack."

Tasha glanced into the back seat. "I know, honey. But you can never do that again. You were very lucky that nothing bad happened."

"I know," Crystal said quietly. "I really do."

"It's over with," Adam said. "But your sister's right. You can't ever run away again."

"I wasn't really running away," Crystal said. "I was going to come back."

"I had no way of knowing that," Tasha told her. "I was so worried."

"I won't do it again, ever, I swear." Crystal sounded sincere.

"Thank you." Tasha turned back to face the front.

"I knew I'd made a mistake the minute I saw Mike, but I was too scared to call you," Crystal explained.

"You can always call me," Tasha said quickly. "Or your Alpha."

Adam was pleased to be included.

The teenager looked up and he saw her eyes in the rearview mirror. "I'm sorry, Alpha. I know I have to be punished but please don't blame Tasha."

Adam tightened his hands on the wheel. "You could have been seriously injured or worse. Not only would that have devastated your sister, but it would have torn the entire Pack apart."

Crystal gasped. "I wasn't thinking."

"No, you weren't. However, I think you've been punished enough," he told her. "That's why I'm taking you to talk to a friend of mine."

Crystal made a face before rubbing her eyes. "I don't need to see a shrink."

Adam chuckled. He would have probably responded the same way. "This woman isn't a shrink. She's the mate to an Alpha who happens to be a very good friend of mine."

The girl looked confused but nodded. "Okay."

Adam smiled at her. "I think you two have a lot in common. You'll be able to talk to her about things you don't to anyone else."

"What things?" she asked suspiciously.

"Marissa is also a non-shifter."

Crystal's eyes widened and her mouth dropped open. "She's a non-shifter and she mated with an Alpha?"

"Yes. Her childhood was pretty rough, but I'll let her tell you about that. The important thing is that you can tell her how you feel and she'll understand." He looked over at Tasha, hoping his words didn't upset her.

Tasha nodded at him. "I think it's a really good idea."

"I guess I could talk to her," Crystal told them.

Yeah, the girl might not want to admit it, but she was dying to speak with someone who might just understand what she was going through.

"We'll be there soon," he promised.

"Have you been before?" Tasha questioned.

"Yes, Gage has been friends with my dad for years. I don't know if you met Logan, but he's been staying at the house because he's my dad's best buddy. My dad is actually staying there now. He left this morning."

"Logan?" she asked. "I don't think I met him."

Tasha touched his arm again. "You're worried about your dad."

Adam glanced in the rearview mirror again before he spoke. Crystal had put on headphones and was bopping around in her seat. He guessed they weren't enough to keep the girl entertained for long. He peered back at Tasha. "Yeah, I am."

Tasha moved her hand up and down his arm. "He'll be okay. Your father was a great Alpha, smart, compassionate and kind. It's no surprise he's struggling with what happened to Mindy and feeling guilty, but he'll see it wasn't his fault. Just give him time."

"I don't know if he has the time," Adam confessed. "I actually hadn't even spoken to him in a week. He could have gotten worse."

"He'll come through this. He was right to turn the Pack over to you and give himself a chance at something else," Tasha said, and the sincerity in her voice squeezed at his heart.

"Thank you," he told her, and meant it more than anything. The tension that had built when he spoke about his father started to drain as they sat in silence. It was nice—the opportunity to sit quietly with someone. While it seemed people at home constantly surrounded him as the Alpha, he could get used to finding solace in Tasha's company.

A short time later, Adam turned onto the paved road that would lead him to the gates to enter Gage's territory. "We're almost there," he told her.

Tasha reached back and jostled Crystal and the teenager pulled off her headphones.

"You have to see the view from here," he said.

The huge wrought-iron gates came into view and an audible gasp came from both women.

"It's so big!" Crystal commented from the back seat.

Adam laughed at the girl's excitement. "Yes. Gage has one of the most beautiful territories."

Tasha shook her head while she stared out of the window. "This is nice, but ours is perfect."

"Yes, it is," he agreed. He hadn't ever wanted to be in such a large Pack. Adam really liked the closeness that came from having small numbers. Adam stopped at the gate and rolled down his window. A young man, no more than twenty, stepped up to the car.

"Hi. Can I help you?" he greeted.

"Yes, I'm Adam White. I believe Gage is expecting us," Adam told him.

The guard smiled and waved to another to let them in. "Yes, Alpha. Gage said to drive right up to the main house."

"Thank you." Adam nodded to the guard. He didn't recognize him, but Logan had already explained that Gage had doubled the guards around the place. First, there'd been an attempted kidnapping attempt on Marissa from her old Pack, then the attacks on the females that had affected Adam's people. With Marissa now expecting the couple's first child, Gage was likely going nuts trying to keep her safe.

The man stepped back and Adam drove through the gate and along the drive. As he pulled up in front of the main house, the front door opened. Gage, Marissa, Logan and Adam's father stepped out and approached the vehicle. Adam opened his door as Gage opened Tasha's and Logan opened Crystal's. After closing the car door, Adam found himself wrapped in his father's arms and lifted off his feet in a strong hug.

Once he was released, Adam looked closely at his father. "You look great." And he did. Christian had been hiding away so Adam had been imagining the worst.

"I *feel* great," his father said, a huge smile on his face.

Adam threw his arm around his father and the two of them walked in front of the car where the others waited.

"I'm glad you made it safely," Gage stated, offering him a hand.

Adam accepted it and bowed his head to the older Alpha. "Thank you for inviting us into your territory."

Gage gave his hand a squeeze before letting go and stepping aside so his mate could greet Adam. Adam bent his head and accepted a kiss on the cheek from the beautiful, pregnant woman.

"Welcome, Alpha Adam," she said softly.

"Thank you," Adam replied, trying to hide the jolt of

surprise at being called Alpha. It still made him feel uneasy sometimes. Especially in front of such a great Alpha as Gage.

Logan stood next to Gage and, pushing his uncomfortable feelings aside, Adam walked up to his father's friend. Instead of shaking his hand, he gave the other man a brief hug and whispered, "Thank you."

Logan patted his back. "You're welcome. I told you he would be okay."

Adam just couldn't believe the change. He hoped Logan was indeed right about Christian already being on the mend and it wasn't that Christian had needed to get away from him and the Pack. It would break Adam's heart if it was his fault it had taken so long for his dad to feel better. Still, he was absolutely thrilled just looking at his father.

Noticing Tasha and Crystal off to the side, Adam motioned them closer. Tasha walked confidently up to him, but Crystal lingered behind.

"Let me introduce you all to two of my favorite Pack members, Tasha and Crystal," Adam said to the group, hoping they would put in extra effort to make the women feel welcome.

Marissa, like a true Alpha's mate, embraced Crystal and held the girl tightly. "I am so glad you're okay, Crystal. Everyone was so worried about you."

Once Marissa had released her, Crystal dropped her head. "I'm sorry for all the trouble I caused." She spoke barely above a whisper.

With her arm still around the teenager, Marissa hushed her. "That's all over now. If I told you how many times I ran away from my Pack—"

"Marissa," Gage warned in a low voice.

Crystal moved closer to Marissa, and Tasha moved closer to Adam. He knew how scary Gage could be in Alpha-mode, but he was also one of the most honorable men Adam had ever met. He wrapped his arm around Tasha's waist while Marissa waved a hand in the air at Gage.

"Oh, stop scaring her." Then she whispered to Crystal, "He thinks he is big and bad, but you should see him reading all the baby books. It's quite adorable."

"Marissa!" Gage snapped at her.

Adam was really getting a good look at what happened when the toughest men he knew fell in love. First Cain and now Gage. It seemed the women were really the ones who ruled.

Adam embraced Tasha harder. He didn't think he'd have a problem with that if he were lucky enough to win Tasha's heart.

Marissa was laughing as she pulled Crystal toward the door. "I'm just saying that maybe you should calm down before you give yourself a stroke. I wasn't going to tell her *everything*."

Gage growled before following her into the house.

Adam held back his laugh until the three disappeared from sight. He wasn't the only one laughing — Tasha, Logan and his father joined him. Wiping a tear from his eye, he looked over at his father, amazed. How long had it been since he'd heard Christian laugh?

"I can hear you three yokels," Gage hollered from the house.

Logan sobered and pointed toward the door. "We should go in before he comes out to get us. Marissa doesn't allow any roughhousing inside so we're much safer in there. He can't retaliate."

"Logan!" Gage yelled. "You want to make a bet on that?"

Biting his lip to keep his amusement inside, Adam led Tasha up the stairs. Gage's Alpha house was three times bigger than his own. Of course, having a smaller Pack meant Adam didn't need as much space. Another thing he was thankful for.

Gage was waiting in the hall for them as they stepped inside.

Logan looked around frantically. "Where's Marissa?"

"She's showing Crystal to one of the spare rooms so she

can get the girl settled and they can talk," Gage said.

"Shit," Logan muttered, then pushed Adam toward Gage.

Surprised, Adam went flying forward from the force of the shove. Gage caught his arm, helping Adam remain on his feet.

"Adam laughed first," Logan accused.

"Really?" Gage let go of Adam's arm as he glared at Logan.

Logan shrugged. "Okay, maybe not. But I bet you really missed me so remember that when you're thinking about burying my body."

Gage sighed, then turned his attention back to Adam. "I only thought I missed him. How much would it cost for you to take him back?"

Adam shook his head. "You don't have enough money." He was both amused and saddened by the play between Gage and his second. Adam really wanted to have that for his own.

"Figures," Gage mumbled. "Come on, I'll show you both to your rooms."

"Uh," Adam glanced back at his dad. As much as he needed a shower, he also didn't want to let his father out of his sight until he'd found out why Christian looked so good.

"Go." Christian waved him on. "We have plenty of time to talk. And we will. I promise."

Adam nodded before holding out his hand to Tasha. She was smiling brightly at him and Adam knew she was just as pleased to see Christian in such good shape as he was.

They followed Gage up the stairs to the second floor. Adam secretly hoped that Tasha's room wasn't too far from his.

* * * *

Adam stepped from the bathroom into the adjoining bedroom in just his towel. The hot water had done a lot to reenergize him. He sat on the bed and picked up his cell to check for messages. He'd already called in to talk to his dad's Beta, whom he'd left in charge. It seemed no one had really missed him.

No emergencies had come up and Adam was relieved. It showed that Logan and everyone else had been right. He didn't have to be available twenty-four hours a day. He could perhaps have a life in addition to running his Pack.

It hadn't been more than a few hours since Adam had been feeling overwhelmed and stuck, but now he was more excited about being the Alpha than ever. He hadn't even felt this good when his father had first broached the subject. He didn't know if any of the positive changes had to do with Tasha, but in his gut, he somehow knew they had.

Her influence and presence in his life just seemed to fit perfectly.

There would be a lot to talk to his dad about. Now that Christian was feeling better, maybe Adam could get his opinion on the possibility of Adam having a relationship with Tasha.

At the knock on his door, Adam turned and strolled to it. Pulling it open, he expected his father but found Tasha outside instead. Her eyes widened before dropping to his waist, reminding him he wasn't dressed. Before he could speak, she licked her lips and his cock jumped beneath the material. She seemed to notice and grinned.

"Tasha," he moaned. His body was reacting to her closeness and his control was on the brink of snapping.

She lifted her hand and ran a finger over the small scar he'd gotten as a child beneath his nipple. He caught her hand in his. Adam was becoming desperate.

"If you come inside, we won't be talking," he warned. He needed her to understand what he craved from her.

Her gaze met his and she smiled. "I hope not. You did promise after all." She pushed him back into his room and closed the door.

Adam stood stunned as she sent him a seductive grin

before reaching for the hem of her shirt and pulling it over her head. He bit his lip to use the pain to ground him. He didn't want to pounce on her and scare her away.

"I have too many clothes on," she announced.

His throat had gone dry so all Adam could do was nod. Tasha ran her slender fingers over the waistband of her pants before pushing them down her hips. When she straightened, she only wore a matching pair of blue panties and bra.

"God, you're beautiful." Adam finally managed to speak. The light colors of her underwear contrasted with her tan skin tone. Adam fisted his hands to keep them off her.

She tossed her hair and laughed. "I could say the same about you. You have a gorgeous body, Alpha."

Her use of his title had Adam's skin cooling. In the past, women of the Pack would offer themselves to the leader as a gift. No Pack he knew of still maintained that practice, but he needed to make sure Tasha didn't think she *had* to give him her body.

"You don't need to do this," he told her, even as regret coursed through his body.

She took several steps. "Oh, yes, I do."

Adam backed away as she continued toward him. "No, you don't. I don't expect anything from you."

She stopped and a thoughtful look crossed her face. And she laughed. "Do you think I'm only sleeping with you because you're my Alpha?"

"I just want to make sure you know that being with me is your choice," he told her honestly. He desired nothing more to than to take her and bury himself as deep inside her as possible, but he wouldn't take it as a 'thank you' for finding her sister. He wanted Tasha to be with him because she just couldn't stand not having him any longer. He needed her to want him as much as he wanted her.

She'd reached him when his legs hit the bed, stopping his retreat. "I get it. Now how can I prove this is something that I want?" Her eyes sparkled with mischief when he met them. She pushed him back hard, where he bounced on the mattress. "Oh, I know!" she said before dropping to her knees in front of him. She yanked off the towel and hummed her approval. "I see that no matter what you say, there is a part of you that wants me."

"All of me wants you," he assured her.

With a firm grip, she wrapped her hand around his ready cock. "I'm glad to hear that," she said, right before engulfing him.

Adam cried out while burying his hands in her hair as she started a strong sucking rhythm. The wet heat that surrounded and teased his cock was almost too much. She used her tongue to massage the sensitive spot directly under the head. Unable to remain still, he bucked against her mouth. "Yes!" He couldn't help lifting his hips off the bed.

Tasha made a sound at the back of her throat, sending vibrations through his cock to the rest of his body. He closed his eyes and just rested back on the bed. She was simply amazing. This strong, independent woman, who knew what she wanted. He found it sexy as hell that she was the one in control.

As Tasha continued to lick and suck him, Adam tightened his hold on her head. He pumped up, sliding his cock over her tongue until the tip brushed the back of her throat. She didn't gag but instead urged him on by sliding her hands under his ass.

Adam braced the soles of his feet on the bed before driving deep again. He only managed five long, slow thrusts before he had to pull back. Tasha chased after his shaft. Not wanting to come before he was inside her, Adam yanked on her hair and held her away from him.

Still on her knees, she gazed up at him. Her lips were glistening and shiny. The sight of her before him was almost too perfect and he could barely keep from shooting his seed. He gripped the base of his cock and squeezed to hold off his climax. When he had control once again, Adam helped her stand with a hand on her arm and turned her until she was bent over the bed.

Tasha was already quivering and moaning.

Adam rubbed and teased her ass before pulling her panties down her legs. She was already wet when he briefly teased her folds. Her scent flooded all of his senses. There was no doubt that she wanted him, that she was ready to take him. He slipped his fingers inside her pussy and she moaned.

He brushed the hair off the back of her neck before he ran his lips over her sensitive skin. Tasha whimpered for more. Adam wanted every sound he could pull from her, wanted to hear her beg. He pumped two fingers in and out of her sex. She lifted her hips and pushed back, drawing his digits even deeper. Each time she pushed back, Adam twisted his hand, driving farther in and making her cry out in ecstasy. Almost desperately, she rode his hand and he knew it was almost time.

They were so consumed with passion that it wouldn't be long before they both exploded. He pulled his fingers from her body and replaced them with the tip of his cock.

"Please, Adam!" she begged. "I want you."

Adam rubbed his cock against her pussy, causing low moans to escape both of them. With shaky hands, he reached around and cupped her breasts through the silk that still covered them. He licked up her spine until he caught the back of her bra in his teeth and ripped the fabric apart.

"Oh!" Tasha cried as he removed the ruined lingerie from her. "Yes!"

"Now it's time to keep my promise."

Tasha pushed back against him, silently telling him she wanted him, too. With one hand pulling on one pert nipple, he moved the other down to play with her clit.

She rubbed shamelessly against him, trying to get enough pressure to make her body tingle. Catching her earlobe between his teeth, he slid both hands along her body to grasp her hips. He bit down, plunging inside. Tasha cried out as he went deep with his first thrust. Licking the small bite, he pulled out and slammed back in.

Tasha wasn't a passive lover. She moved into each stroke and met him in every way. Her hot body accepted and milked him each time he withdrew and entered again. Adam had to hold on tight or risk being bucked off. It was amazing.

As Adam drove them high with his frantic thrusts, sweat began to cover their bodies. His hand slid off her breasts so he gripped her shoulder while still toying with her clit. Tasha's sounds were growing in volume and spurring him on.

Each time he plunged his cock into her tight pussy, her inner muscles clamped down on him. He knew they were only seconds away from going over the edge.

Adam withdrew from her body.

"No!" Tasha screeched.

"Turn over," he ordered. He wanted to be looking in her eyes when he came.

She complied quickly, twisting on the mattress so she was on her back. Adam pushed her thighs apart before grasping his cock.

"Tell me I can come inside you," he requested.

"Yes!" she insisted. "I'm on birth control."

Shifters couldn't carry or pass on disease, so the only time he wore a condom with another shifter was when they had to worry about pregnancy. He hadn't even thought about putting on a rubber or asking before he'd buried his shaft inside her.

"Thank God," Adam murmured.

He leaned forward again so that he could slide the tip of his cock through her folds. "Kiss me."

She raised her head and their lips met.

Adam licked and nipped until she opened up and he could push his tongue inside her mouth. At the same time, he drove his shaft forward.

Tasha screamed, but he swallowed the sound.

He continued to drive his hips hard and fast until she tightened around him. Her nails scored down his back as she climaxed.

He hissed but didn't slow down or stop. Instead, he slid his hands under her butt and lifted her until he was able to mindlessly push his cock deep. Sweat dripped from his forehead onto her chest, but she still clung to him.

Adam threw back his head and howled as he came hard. He was panting and shaking, but even though completely sated, he didn't want to slip out of Tasha's body quite yet. Instead, he rolled until she lay on his chest.

"Wow," Tasha said in awe.

Adam chuckled. Yeah, that had been pretty awesome. He couldn't wait to do it again, and again and again.

Chapter Four

Tasha woke up with a hard, warm body pressed up against her back. With a small smile, she snuggled against it, feeling Adam's morning erection dig into her bottom. Moving her hips in a slow side-to-side motion, she was treated to Adam wrapping his arm around her and pulling her tighter to him.

"Good morning, baby," he whispered huskily next to her ear.

Her heart swelled at the endearment — one she had never been called before. "Morning."

He started thrusting his hips against her so she reached around and took hold of his erection. With her thumb, she teased the slit of his cock, releasing a small pearl of liquid.

"Oh, God, you have such great hands," he told her, rolling her onto her back and taking possession of her mouth.

He brushed his tongue forcefully over her lips was until she opened for him. Tasha loved his flavor. A hint of spice and something wild. Even this early in the morning, she wouldn't want anything to mask his natural taste. Tasha sucked on his tongue as Adam stroked his palms all over her body.

Their tongues dueled, caressing, as his body covered hers. Adam kissed down her neck until he reached her breasts. Tasha arched her back when he took one hard nipple into his mouth and sucked. Tasha cried out in ecstasy.

"I love your breasts. So full and soft," he whispered against her skin.

Tasha had always hated how big they were. They had been a cause of teasing as she'd gotten older and filled out before the other girls. But, with Adam worshipping them in the most loving way, for the first time, she was proud of them.

When Adam started to move down her body once again, she grabbed his hair, trying to pull him back up. He just chuckled and drove his tongue into her belly button.

Tasha had never thought that was an erogenous zone, but with him lavishing it with care, she found herself bucking under him. By the time he reached her plumped folds, she was ready to scream at him to take her. Then his skilled fingers separated her wet folds and he pushed one digit inside.

"Oh!" She panted as he pumped in and out. She lifted her hips to give him better access and he inserted a second finger. Tasha rode his hand until his mouth covered her swollen clit and he sucked.

She exploded, crying out his name. Adam stopped tasting her, instead working her body until she was grasping desperately at the sheets. Her breathing labored, she tried to speak, but he was once again making his way up her body, leaving a trail of moisture from his tongue and her own juices.

When he covered her and bent his head, he shared her unique taste before starting to push that wonderfully long cock inside. Tasha planted her feet on the bed and lifted her hips to help him inside. In one hard, deep thrust, he entered her.

Her muscles tightened and gripped him. He was longer than any other man she'd been with, but he fit perfectly in the most intimate way. While he slammed inside her, Tasha scratched at his shoulders. He pounded into her with a rhythm so fast a normal man could never reach it. Before she knew it, she was once again riding another wave of ecstasy.

He grabbed her legs and hooked them over his shoulders. His strokes grew desperate. Three, four, and five more times he rammed into her and came hard, his deep voice echoing around the room.

As he collapsed on her, Tasha ran her hands through his hair, wanting to hold on to every second she had with this very special man. In the short time they'd been together, Adam had made her feel better than anyone else had in her life. His concern for her sister was only a small part of why she admired him. She had never been comfortable in the company of a lot of people. She had always been a loner. It was easier to hide her and her family's problems that way. But Adam had the ability to draw her from her shell. First, in the city, and now, in another Pack's territory.

Try as she might, she couldn't keep her mind from moving into the future and taunting her with pictures of her and Adam together...in a more permanent situation. She held him tighter. Tasha knew she could never be the mate to the Alpha. She wasn't pretty or smart and she didn't have the right connections. She was just a lost woman with the responsibilities of raising a child. A teenager who was going through something that Tasha didn't have a clue about how to help her with. She kind of hoped that Adam would have some ideas, like bringing Crystal to Marissa, but she couldn't rely on him to fix all her problems. Adam didn't need that kind of pressure. He had enough on his shoulders without taking care of her burdens, too.

In her heart, Tasha knew she'd have to let him go once they left to return home. So, right now, she would hang on as long as she could.

"We should probably get out of bed and shower," Adam said.

"Ugh," Tasha managed. She didn't want to. "We could take a nap."

"We're going to need to eat eventually," Adam said with a laugh.

Now that he'd mentioned it, Tasha was starving. She dropped her arms from his body, but instead of standing, Adam propped himself up on an elbow to peer down at her.

"What?" she asked, wanting to squirm under his direct look.

"We'll need to head back soon," Adam said.

All the contentment faded. She should have held on tighter. "I know."

"So when we get back home, I want to take you on a real date," he said. "Dinner at a nice restaurant, a movie, a midnight stroll."

Tasha sucked in a breath. He wanted to keep seeing her?

"Would that be okay with you?" He watched her closely.

She nodded, incapable of words.

"But first, I was hoping you'd run with me today," he said. "I'd like to let my wolf out before the long drive back and I was wondering if you'd come with me."

Tasha blinked at him as she digested the words. Never before had she shifted with a male and let their wolves bond. It was an intimate act she hadn't been lucky enough to ever believe would be possible.

"Tasha?" Adam's features changed to concerned, then sad. "You don't have to." He started to lift off her, but she quickly wrapped her arms and legs around him.

"Yes!" She practically screamed the word.

Adam froze.

"Yes," she repeated. "I want that so much."

"Really?" he asked. "You seemed surprised."

"I didn't...I haven't ever..."

"Me, neither," Adam assured her. "But I want to with you."

This was happening so fast. Tasha's head spun. "Are you sure?"

When Adam pulled back and sat up Tasha didn't stop him this time. Instead, she climbed out of bed and stood in front of him. Adam wasn't looking at her and she didn't know what she'd said wrong.

"Hey." She grabbed his chin.

"You never have to do anything you don't want to," he whispered.

And now they were back to his insecurities, which meant Tasha was going to have to let go of hers. She might fear that Adam was caught up in excitement, but that didn't mean she shouldn't take his feelings into consideration.

"I'll make you a deal," she said.

Adam narrowed his eyes.

"I'll accept that you really want me. It's seems unbelievable that you find me attractive, but I won't question your feelings. But you have to stop thinking that all my decisions have to do with you being the Alpha," she said.

He snorted. "I way more than find you attractive. I can feel something growing between us, don't you?"

"Yes," she confessed. "I feel it, too. I just don't know if I can trust it, though."

"If not" — he rose before reaching for her — "you can trust me."

Tasha smiled at him. "I trust you."

"Good, we need to find out how far we can go together," he said. "Give me, give us, a chance."

It was all she wanted in the world. Years of watching and wishing didn't even compare to what it was really like to be with Adam. And she was telling the truth — it had nothing to do with him being the Alpha. She could remember the first time she'd really seen him. It had been the summer she'd turned fifteen. Her mom and dad had been fighting and Crystal had been with a neighbor. Tasha had walked down to the creek in the middle of the territory. The older boys had been there, swimming and playing.

Tasha had hidden behind a tree and watched.

Adam, always the ringleader of trouble, had been jumping off one of the high ridges, butt naked. It hadn't been the first time she'd see a male nude. Shifting as part of the Pack had made nudity common, but still, Tasha had found herself following every one of Adam's curves and twitch of muscles. He had been spectacular and time had only increased how hot he'd grown.

"Where'd you go just now?" Adam's words pulled her

from her memory.

"Nowhere," she said. The past wasn't something she wanted to get into right then. "I was just remembering something."

Adam caressed her face. "Okay."

"So do we have a deal?" she asked. "We both let go of our insecurities?"

"If you run with me."

Tasha laughed. "Deal."

* * * *

Adam led Tasha to the living room with a hand on the small of her back. He was making no secret of the two of them having been together the night before and that morning. It was his claim and he was just getting started. She'd been right earlier. He needed to stop thinking that everyone only wanted something from the Alpha. Adam was surrounded by good people and they weren't trying to use him. He needed to trust people and that would start with Tasha. And it would begin here in the home of an amazing Alpha.

As they entered the large room, they found Crystal curled up on the end of the brown leather couch. She was leaning over, whispering to Marissa, her head bent. Adam made his way to the other side of his room where his father stood to allow Tasha to keep going to the young girl.

When she saw Tasha, Crystal jumped up and ran to her, throwing her arms around her neck. "Did you know that when Marissa was my age she got kicked out of a Pack for being a non-shifter? And that she ran to the city, too? She didn't even know that a non-shifter could mate with a shifter and have babies!"

That was a lot of information at once. Tasha smiled at Crystal, listening intently. "I didn't know that," she answered the teenager.

Crystal held on to her hand and tugged her toward the

couch. "And it wasn't until she came here for her sister's mating ceremony and met Gage that she learned the truth. She had been living all by herself without any Pack for years."

Listening to Crystal explain things to Tasha made Adam realize that even though they loved everyone equally, they weren't educating the young as they should be. Adam knew about non-shifters from his father, but that didn't mean the rest of the Pack shared the same knowledge. Crystal was opening his eyes to one place he needed to start making his mark.

"We never shunned non-shifters, but we didn't show them they were accepted, either," Christian whispered.

Adam nodded. "I was just thinking that. I have an idea."

"Good," Christian clasped his shoulder. "I knew you would do good things."

He only nodded distantly as he listened to the women talk.

"That must have been terrible," Tasha said to Marissa. "I couldn't even imagine."

Marissa laughed and waved a hand in the air. "Oh, it was. But if I had to do it again to make my way here to Gage, I would."

Adam believed Marissa. The bond between Gage and Marissa was one of the strongest he'd ever witnessed.

Tasha stroked her sister's back silently and Adam really wanted to go to them and comfort them both. Crystal told Tasha about how Marissa had a lot of the same feelings as she did. And that she could also feel the wolf inside her at times.

"Wait!" Tasha interrupted. "You never told me you could feel your wolf."

Crystal dropped her gaze and Tasha quickly looked over to Marissa. Marissa shifted so she could place her hand on Crystal's arm.

"I never told my older sister, either," Marissa explained. "I didn't know how."

Tasha threw her arms around the girl's shoulder and hugged her tightly. "You can tell me anything, sweetheart. But I understand that you were scared."

"I didn't know what was wrong with me. I know I can't shift, so shouldn't that mean I don't have a wolf inside me?"

Adam walked over to the couch and placed his hand on Crystal's shoulder. "You shouldn't have gone through this on your own. I'll help make sure that no one else feels as alone as you did."

"I'm lucky," Crystal told him. "I have Tasha. Even after my mom and dad left, I always had my sister. And Tasha has always accepted me."

"We all accept you," Adam said.

"It's amazing, now I know that I do have the wolf inside. She's trapped on the inside just like I am on the outside." Crystal's eyes cleared and Adam could see the excitement. "Marissa runs with Gage."

A laugh had Adam looking over at Marissa, who clarified, "Well, obviously not *now*, but before. The wild animal is inside us just the same. To run, to feel the wind, does magical things."

Crystal laughed, too. "Well, she would run in human form. She can run faster than a normal human. I think that's because of the wolf inside. By running, she's letting her wolf out a little."

Adam nodded because it did make sense.

"So I want to try that. I want to run with the wolves!" Tasha announced loudly.

"You want to run with the wolves?" he asked. This was absolutely the best timing.

Crystal nodded. "Marissa said I have to start slowly. Just run a little and I can work up to a mile and then more."

Adam caught Tasha's eye and she shrugged.

If he allowed Crystal to accompany them on the run, it wouldn't be long before Crystal would have to head back inside. He and Tasha would still have plenty of time to let their wolf halves bond. Crouching down in front of them,

Adam took Tasha's hand, then Crystal's. "How about if you start going for a run with me and your sister? That way we can keep an eye on you if you get tired."

Crystal let out a cry and threw her arms around him. "Thank you! Thank you!"

He hugged the girl back. Adam knew he was doing the right thing. This feeling inside him was one that he wanted to have last all the time. He'd get that wish if he kept doing right by his Pack. "You're very welcome."

Adam released the teen and strolled back over to his dad, who was grinning widely. Adam couldn't get over the change in his father.

"Good job," Christian praised.

"I learned from the best," Adam told him.

Christian shook his head. "You'll be a better Alpha than me. That's the hope for all of my generation. That our children succeed where we failed."

"You didn't fail," Adam said.

"Maybe not," Christian replied. "But I let people down. You being one of them."

Adam started to argue, but Christian held up his hand. "Logan was right. Instead of being scared that I would disappoint you, I should have talked to you. I'm sorry."

"I don't want you to be sorry." Adam gripped his father's hand. "I just want my dad back."

"I hope you'll always feel that way."

He didn't understand what his dad meant. "Why wouldn't I?"

Christian smiled. "Come see me later, after you've taken the girls on the run. We have some things to discuss."

"Sure," Adam agreed. He didn't like where this conversation seemed to be headed. He'd been convinced that his dad was healing, but now it seemed as though Christian had bad news for him. "As long as everything is okay."

"Everything is the way it is supposed to be," Christian said. "I believe that with all my heart."

"Okay," Adam turned back to the women. "Who's ready to go on a run?"

As Tasha walked with Adam to the secluded spot Gage had told them about, her stomach fluttered with butterflies. It wasn't just the thought of her sister running with her for the first time that had her so nervous, but knowing Adam would be right beside her the entire run.

Adam held her hand until they reached their destination. He turned toward her and brought her hand up to his mouth. He kissed the back before turning it over and nipping her wrist. "I can sense your uneasiness," he said gently.

She laughed. "I feel like this is my first date or something."

Adam was grinning. "Our first date will come when we get home. This is just a prelude. Besides, you have to admit this is beautiful land."

It was. Tasha had always thought that this western part of Texas was nothing but dry land and dead trees. Instead, Gage's territory was lush with green turf and healthy vegetation. They didn't have the mountains or the ridges of home, but it was still pretty.

Even though she was grateful she was going to get this opportunity, she really wanted to shift with Adam in their own territory, so she was looking at this as a trial until they got home.

"This is going to be fun," Adam said. "I promise."

"I'm ready."

Adam leaned forward to brush his lips over hers. Tasha gripped him by the nape of the neck so when he would have pulled away, she instead deepened the kiss. She thrust her tongue inside his mouth while bringing his body close to hers.

She started to grow lightheaded, but it was Adam who pulled back. He was panting.

"I now have to shift with a hard-on," he told her. "Thanks for that."

She giggled, wow, actually giggled.

"Come on." Adam grabbed her hand before yanking her behind a tree. "Let's shift. I'm going to make you pay for that kiss later."

Tasha looked forward to it. She followed suit when Adam began to undress. When they were both nude, he nodded at her.

"Go ahead," he said.

Tasha crouched but kept her gaze on his as she called forth her wolf. The magic seemed to swirl around her until her body began the transformation. There was no pain, no sound of breaking bones, or anything like she'd read about. Instead, the entire change only took minutes and was pretty seamless. She had been a human and now as she rose on her paws, she looked like every other wolf in the wild.

She rolled her neck before stretching her back. Tasha didn't shift often. It didn't seem right when she knew Crystal would never have the ability. She tried to make the full-moon runs when the Pack did them, but it had been several months since anyone had organized a full Pack activity. It must have been three or four months ago since she'd last transformed.

Because she didn't shift as often as some of her friends, Tasha wondered if she were missing out on the connection to her animal. She'd overheard several of the Pack and how they talked about their wolves.

Adam finished his own transformation. Wow, she hadn't seen him shift in a while, but even she didn't think he'd been that big of a wolf before. Must be an Alpha thing. He was yawning while trying to scratch his ear.

She trotted over and starting licking at his muzzle. Adam rolled over onto his back, enjoying her attention. Once she'd lavished attention on every inch of his face, he flipped back to his stomach, then stood. He shook his massive body. Tasha rubbed her side against his, mingling their scents together.

Adam raised his head and howled. Tasha felt the pull of

her Alpha and gave an answering cry.

When he took off at a sprint, she scrambled behind him. She caught up quickly — no doubt he let her — and she gave herself over to her animal instincts. The wind carried her body as she leaped over a fallen log and landed flawlessly next to Adam. He ate up the ground with his long strides. A perfect blend of muscle and power covered in a thick black pelt. Her smaller body ran hard to keep up with his longer legs. She felt free running beside him.

He nipped her shoulder and turned her to the east, no doubt leading her back to the spot where her sister would be waiting. A selfish part of her wanted to continue to run with him and be alone together.

She scolded herself and focused instead on her sister, but she couldn't help it. Giving in to her instincts was bringing her desire for him closer to the surface. In human form, it was easier to push aside her own wants.

That was what she should be doing — looking out for her sister. Tasha tucked her head and picked up speed. As they raced back toward the house, the freedom of the running lifted her spirits. Adam led the way to the meeting spot and she only slowed when she caught the scent of her sister. All her senses were heightened. She could practically taste her sister's excitement mixed with nerves as they drew closer. Adam stopped running several feet away from the group so she followed suit. Soon, they stood among the three in human form.

Crystal walked slowly to Tasha and ran a hand through the fur that covered her neck. Tasha leaned against her sister, letting her know she enjoyed the touch. The teenager let out a cry of delight and dropped to her knees, throwing her arms around her. It was only then that Tasha realized that she had never taken her other form around her sister. She'd always been so careful not to rub in the fact that Crystal couldn't shift. Adam nuzzled her from the other side and she felt truly loved in that moment.

They waited until Crystal stood, taking a deep breath prior

to starting to run before they took off after her. Adam kept a slow pace behind Crystal so Tasha began running beside her. Crystal's breathing came hard as she ran through the thick grass, deep into the woods.

Tasha was trying to come up with a way to stop her when Adam raced in front of them, blocking their way. Almost in perfect order, Crystal and Tasha stopped next to him. The young girl bent at the waist with her hands on her knees, drawing in long gulps of air. When she looked up and over at Tasha, the smile on her face made Tasha's heart sing.

This was something they could share, to bring them closer. Instead of hiding a part of herself from Crystal, Tasha would be able to have a way for the two of them to connect. It was a precious gift.

Marissa jogged up and, even pregnant, she moved flawlessly. She might not have been able to shift, but Tasha could still feel the wolf inside her. Tasha turned toward her sister and concentrated.

There, a small smell of woods and wild animal. Tasha crept forward and ran her snout around Crystal's stomach to her lower back. It wasn't as noticeable as Marissa's, but Tasha could pick up that there was a wolf inside Crystal.

"Can you feel it?" Crystal asked. "I can! I'm a shifter, too."

Tasha nodded. She might have always told Crystal that she was accepted and loved, but Tasha hadn't known what the teen was going through. Gage and Marissa had helped so much already and it was all due to Adam's influence. She nuzzled Crystal's hand before plodding over to Adam. He nestled his snout into her neck.

"Why don't the two of you finish your run?" Marissa suggested.

Tasha looked over at the young woman.

"I'll take care of Crystal. We still have some things to talk about before you all leave," Marissa said.

"I'll be fine," Crystal said. "Go, enjoy the rest of your run."

Adam nudged her, so Tasha let herself be led away. It had been amazing to have Crystal involved in this part of her life, but now it was time to really let go.

Tasha waited until they were out of sight of her sister, then took off in a full run. Adam pounded behind her, but that was what she wanted. She might be smaller but that also meant that she had a pretty good chance of outrunning him.

She leaped over large rocks and fallen tree limbs, hoping the addition of the obstacles would slow Adam down. It didn't seem to be working, since she could still feel his breath on her flank. She didn't want to lose him, only make it into a real chase.

The leaves crunched under her paws and she could smell water close by. A perfect place to end the pursuit.

Tasha took a sharp right and Adam flew past her. He was scrambling to change direction and follow, but she had surprised him. With the last burst of energy, she sprinted as fast as she could. The cool blue of the water reflected her and she slowed down. The canopy above her blocked out the sun and it was chilly here. She wheezed from the hard pace, so she dipped her head and drank deeply.

Once her thirst was sated, she looked up and saw Adam's large wolf form grinning at her. She shook her head. It seemed she hadn't lost him after all.

Tasha began her transformation back to human and Adam saw, leading him to do the same. When she was human again, Tasha kneeled up. Adam was already human, his shift taking half the time as hers.

"Why don't you come closer?" she asked.

Adam grinned. "Stand up for me."

She complied, curious where this was going. "Now what?"

He tilted his head toward the creek. "Go ahead."

Tasha frowned. The water looked cold. "I don't think so."

"No?" Adam teased. Then he rose, winked at her and jumped. The splash was big and some drops landed on her arm.

Well, if he could handle the cold water, so could she.

Tasha put a foot in the edge and quickly pulled it back out. "Are you kidding me? It's freezing!"

"Oh, don't be such a baby," he called.

Tasha narrowed her eyes. "What did you call me?"

"You're nothing but a big baby," Adam said.

No, he didn't. Tasha took several steps back, then ran forward and leaped in. She made sure to land close enough to Adam to soak him. He was laughing as she popped up above the surface.

Jeez, it was even colder than she'd first thought. Why had she let him taunt her into this?

Adam swam closer to wrap his arm around her waist so that her body pressed to his. With the temperature of the water, she was surprised to feel his cock hard against his thigh.

"Really?" She raised an eyebrow.

"What can I say?" he asked. "I want you."

Tasha grinned. "Prove it."

Chapter Five

Adam glanced at his watch. It was only a few hours after dinner and he wanted to speak to his father before it got too late. Christian had been looking so well earlier, but as they'd eaten, he'd seemed preoccupied and worried. Adam hoped nothing was going wrong. He'd been so excited that his dad was happy and healthy. Somehow Logan and Gage's territory had soothed Christian and Adam was going to do everything in his power to make sure his father made it through this trial.

He quickly made his way to his father's room, knowing Christian had been turning in early. Still resting, Logan had told Adam.

Instead of knocking, he walked into the bedroom like he'd always done and found a sight that shocked him to the core. His father had his arms locked around Logan as they shared a deep, intimate kiss. The two broke away when Adam entered.

Adam squinted. His eyes must be betraying him.

"Adam, close the door," his father told him quietly.

He would have loved to, but the shock and confusion that clouded his mind kept him from moving. Christian hadn't let go of Logan.

"Adam!" his father snapped and, like a curtain lifting, his vision cleared.

There was his father, the greatest man he had ever known, standing shoulder to shoulder with another man, who was obviously his lover. There was no doubt in Adam's mind that they were lovers. Logan's scent was all over his father's room. All over his father. This hadn't been a one-time incident. And why had he never noticed that before? Sure, he had been busy, but something like his dad taking a lover should have been extremely obvious. That could only mean that his father had taken great pains to ensure Adam hadn't found out.

His dad didn't trust him, was keeping secrets from him.

Adam grew lightheaded. How much of his life had he screwed up? He just wanted to be a good Alpha. To show his dad that Adam was going to take care of his legacy. But Christian obviously didn't think Adam could be trusted with really important matters, like Christian's love life.

Adam's eyes burned with tears. The ridge between his father and him might be too large to come back from.

A sharp pain in his chest had him gasping. All his hard work and he'd lost his dad.

Christian took a step forward and Adam panicked. "Stay back!" he ordered. He felt so hurt, so betrayed.

"Close the door and we'll talk about this," his father assured him calmly.

"Talk? You want to talk about this?" he questioned, his voice rising above his normal tone. "Now?"

"Yes, talk. Like adults, which the three of us are."

He jerked, feeling as if he'd just been slapped. His father was reprimanding *him*? What was happening? He was an Alpha now, but his father had turned his back on Adam.

"Yes, we are adults." The cool, calm voice couldn't have come from his mouth. Not with the way his body shook. "Although it doesn't look to me as though the two of you do much talking."

His father didn't pull his gaze from Adam's. "I was going to explain—"

Adam barked out a bitter laugh. "Explain? Why would you need to explain anything to me? Keeping Logan here as your little dark secret is your own business."

Christian's eyes flashed. "You will not disrespect him." His voice rose, as well.

Adam turned on his heel and stalked out of the door. "I

don't have to respect him, either, neither of you." With the last word, he slammed the door behind him and headed toward the back of the house.

Lucky no one was around, since Adam felt inclined to bite the head off any person who stood between him and his freedom, because the only thing he knew for sure was that he had to get out of the house. His long, angry strides ate up the distance until he stood once again at the edge of the woods. He quickly tore off his clothes and knelt, calling to his brother wolf. With a cry of anguish, he let the magic sweep over his body and, for the second time of the day, changed into his other form. The wolf wanted to run. To get away from the worry, the doubt, the pain that he felt.

Without someone else slowing him down, he took off.

Why wouldn't his dad tell him that he'd fallen for Logan? It was an amazing thing and Christian should be proud. The two men would make one hell of a team. Even if Christian didn't want anything to do with Adam, then at least he would have a strong partner at his back. Adam wouldn't have to worry about his father. Christian could get a new start with a new Pack or Logan could join theirs. Adam was looking for strong shifters to fill his inner circle. Logan would have fitted in perfectly, but if Christian and Logan couldn't even talk to him about their relationship, they must not trust his judgement.

Adam had never felt more alone in his life. Not even after he'd lost his mom.

He spotted a narrow trail and, even though he didn't know where it would lead, he changed direction toward it. If he were in his own territory, he'd head for his favorite ridge. The place that allowed him to look over his own land.

There were people whom he'd left behind who needed him. Even if Christian was no longer trusting Adam's judgement, that didn't mean that Adam was going to turn his back on those who did need him.

The trail was taking him deeper into the woods and, as the area surrounding him darkened, he began to calm.

He always felt better when he spent time in nature. Now that the territory belonged to him, the more time he spent roaming the land would help soothe him when he was tied up in knots.

If Christian needed space from Adam, then that was something he could give his father. Adam was still his son, wanted to make his dad proud. Maybe it would be easier if they were hundreds of miles apart.

Adam needed to collect Tasha and Crystal and get them home. In time, he'd try to mend the fences with his father.

He must have run for over an hour. Adam had enough sense to stay within the Pack territory but went as far from the main house as he could. It wasn't until he was completely exhausted that he stopped and collapsed next to an old, tall oak tree. His heart hurt more than his body.

The shift back came slowly, but sooner than he wanted. Once again in human form, he sat naked with his back against the tree. He heard his visitor before he saw her.

"Go away," he ordered and hoped she would listen. Adam just needed a little more time to get his head on straight. Just peace and quiet.

Instead of doing as she'd been told, Tasha stepped into view with her hands on her hips. Oh, this wasn't what he needed.

"Don't you bark orders out at me! Do you know how long I have been trying to follow you?" she asked.

Adam couldn't help it. He laughed. It started with just a chuckle and grew until he had to put his hand on his stomach to calm himself down. Here he was, pouting in the middle of the woods, and his lover was reprimanding him. His life was turning into a huge mess, but Tasha was pulling him from his hurt.

The entire time, Tasha stood in the same pose, frustration evident in her expression.

Adam waved a hand in front of his face as he gathered his senses.

"I'm so happy you find me funny," she remarked, but her

lips twitched as if she were holding in a laugh.

"I'm not fit for company right now," he warned. He didn't want to screw things up with her, too. "Go back to the house and I'll return shortly."

When he didn't hear any movement, he looked over. She was still there.

"No," she replied simply, then walked forward and knelt in front of him. She lifted a hand to his face, but he caught her wrist.

"I'm not having a good night," he said. "Just let me be."

"No."

Adam only grunted in response. She was a stubborn woman, but that was one of the things he liked best about her.

Tasha came even closer until she was almost straddling him. "Well, let's change that, why don't we?"

He shook his head. "I'm not in the mood."

"Really?" She lifted an eyebrow before grabbing the hem of her shirt. She whipped the garment over her head. "Guess I'll just leave you alone."

The words were barely out of her mouth when he pounced. She fell back and collided with the solid ground as his body covered hers. He slammed his mouth on hers, demanding entrance. When she didn't open fast enough, he bit her lower lip, causing her to gasp. Adam thrust his tongue inside, dominating everything he could. The blood in his body burned and throbbed as he situated himself between her legs. His cock pressed against the zipper of her jeans when he ground himself against her, showing her that he wasn't playing games. He was already naked.

He ripped his mouth from hers when she pushed back against him. Adam stared down at her abused lips. Guilt flooded him immediately. "I can't be gentle with you right now. I don't want to do it this way and hurt you."

Tasha launched herself up and attached her mouth to his neck. She sucked his skin into her mouth while running her nails down his back. He hissed and arched from the slight bite of pain.

"I don't want gentle. I want you to take me right here and now. Fuck me, Adam," she whispered in his ear.

God help him, he couldn't resist her. She had given him permission to use her, to ride her hard, and he wasn't going to pass that up. He pushed her back down and quickly went about removing her clothes. She lifted her hips to help him pull down her pants, then reached and removed her bra as he yanked off her panties.

"You're going to have to start buying me new underwear if you keep doing that," she teased.

Adam growled and buried his face in her stomach. "Shouldn't wear any ever again." His response came out muffled.

He tried to slow himself down, but he could smell the heat and juices from her sweet pussy. She was just as hot as he was. The wolf inside was almost at the surface and the animal wanted to come out to play.

"Adam…" Tasha wriggled under him.

He pulled back and settled more firmly between her legs. Cupping her bottom, he lifted her up and brought her hot core to the tip of his hard shaft. He was going to give it to her hard, but he wanted her to enjoy it, as well.

"Look at me," he demanded. "Watch me as I take you. As I fuck you any way I want."

Her eyes widened, her breath quickened and she nodded. His words were obviously turning her on.

Adam plunged inside with a howl, catching her scream by slamming his mouth down on hers.

Tasha's inner muscles squeezed and tried to hold him inside, causing Adam to close his eyes and wait. The peacefulness that overtook his body now that he was buried inside threatened to bring tears to his eyes.

"Adam." Tasha reached up to brush the hair of his forehead.

Adam opened his eyes and saw her smile. "It feels like home."

Tasha nodded in response to his declaration. "I feel it, too."

Adam started to withdraw from her but thought better. He leaned down and kissed her with all the passion and love he felt. Tasha opened for him immediately. When she lifted her head to deepen the kiss, he nipped her bottom lip.

"I have to move now, baby," he told her honestly.

Tasha's response was to lift her legs higher around his waist. "Get busy."

He laughed as he pulled out and slammed back in. Her breath stuttered and he did it again. Adam started with long, deep strokes, trying to draw out both their pleasures.

Anger and confusion no longer ate at him. Now it was only the need to take care of his woman.

Tasha's nails dug into his shoulders and he continued to plunge inside her, but it wasn't enough for him. He quickly left the hot haven of her body to flip her onto her stomach. She was barely in position before he grabbed her hips and thrust back inside. He rode her hard, enjoying the small sounds escaping her lips. When her body began to tremble, he reached around and rubbed her clit.

"Yes," she moaned.

Adam continued to play with her until his balls drew up. Knowing climax was only seconds away, he pinched her clit hard. She screamed before exploding. Adam followed her into release, his seed filling her, before they both collapsed forward.

Tasha recovered first and wiggled out from under Adam. He wrapped his arm around her, shifting onto his side. Her sigh was enough to calm his beating heart.

"That was great," she said dreamily.

Adam laughed. "It was that, indeed."

She crawled up until she was resting her head on his chest. "Are you feeling better now?"

He couldn't resist. Adam lazily ran his hand over her bottom, delighting in the shivers he caused. "I feel great," he commented.

Tasha giggled before slapping his chest. "I meant about what happened earlier in the house."

Adam removed his hand and started to sit up. "How much did you hear?" he asked.

Tasha dropped her gaze and reached for her pants. "Everyone heard quite a bit, but your dad told me the rest."

Adam cursed and started to move her away. "I screwed up. I don't know how, but my dad doesn't trust me."

"No! Your father loves you. He's so proud of you."

He snorted. "Yeah, right."

"Just because he hadn't told you about Logan doesn't mean—"

"Doesn't mean what?" Adam snapped. "That he is hiding his relationship from me?"

"I'm sure he had his reasons," Tasha said.

"Yeah." That was the problem, wasn't it?

"You should talk to him," Tasha suggested. "Just hash things out once and for all."

"I can't," Adam confessed. It pained him to say the words.

"Why not?"

"I can't stand to see the disappointment on his face again," Adam told her.

"What disappointment?"

"He doesn't think I'm doing a good job running the Pack," Adam said. "He's sorry he turned it over to me."

Tasha laughed.

He jerked back as if he'd been slapped.

"I'm sorry." She giggled. "That couldn't be further from the truth."

"So why hasn't he told me about Logan?"

"He was scared," she said.

"Scared of what?"

She narrowed her eyes. "You dad's life is changing. He gave up his position of Alpha up. He's fallen in love with a man. Someone who'd been his friend his entire life. If he'd told you about Logan, it would have made their relationship real, and if he and Logan don't work out, he'll lose that friendship."

Adam sat stunned. He hadn't even considered the fact that his father was dealing with uncertain feelings. He'd been so wrapped up in his own insecurities he'd majorly dropped the ball. He'd said such horrible things to both his dad and Logan.

"Fuck."

Tasha shook his head. "You get it now?"

"I get it."

"So, does that mean you're okay with your father and Logan?" Tasha asked.

"Of course. I just want him to be happy."

"Maybe you should tell him that," she suggested.

Adam smiled. "I will, right away." He wrapped his arms around her waist. "Thank you."

Tasha's grin brightened her face. "I'm so relieved. Everyone here is so great and...I really like Logan."

Adam nodded. "So do I. He's always been a great friend to my father. I probably shouldn't be surprised their relationship turned into more. They do make a handsome couple."

"They're both dreamboats." Tasha climbed off his lap and this time he let her. "So are you ready to go back?"

He watched her shimmy into her clothes. "Yeah, we'd better go in before they send out a bigger search party."

Tasha hummed, smiling. "Just don't greet them the same way."

He was amused, loving the playful side she was sharing with him. "Get dressed, my little minx."

"I wanted to talk to you about Crystal," she said once she was ready to leave.

"She okay?" he asked worried.

"I was talking to Marissa and she suggested that Crystal stay a couple of weeks."

"Stay here?"

"Yeah," Tasha said. "Crystal doesn't have to be at school for another month. Marissa wants to show her the new chat room set up for non-shifter teenagers that she oversees. I guess Marissa has several programs in place to make sure what happened to her doesn't ever happen again."

"That's great," Adam told her. "It would give us a chance to come back up here. I don't want to lose touch with my dad. Show him and Logan that I support them."

"That's a wonderful idea," Tasha said. "It will give Crystal the opportunity to spend some more time with Marissa while giving you a reason to return here."

"I'll discuss this with Gage." Adam nodded at the Alpha who stood at the exit of the woods.

"Well." Tasha laughed. "I guess I'll let you too talk."

By the glare on Gage's face, Adam wasn't really looking forward to hearing whatever the Alpha had to say. Tasha had said that everyone had heard the fight. It couldn't really be a surprise that Gage was going to come to his Beta's defense.

Gage nodded to Tasha as she passed him, while Adam stopped walking. He waited until Gage had almost reached him before he acknowledged the other Alpha.

"You okay?"

"Yeah," Adam answered, surprised. He had expected Gage to be angry, not wearing a look of concern. "You knew," he accused but without the anger he'd felt earlier.

Gage nodded. "I suspected. They still haven't *told* me, but it's not something that you miss when you are with them every day."

Adam shook his head. "I should have been paying better attention."

"No," Gage said. "You have your hands full. A new Alpha and this problem with Crystal. It's understandable."

"He's my dad," Adam said.

"So Christian knows how to hide things from you," Gage said.

"Yeah."

"Do you know what you're going to say?" Gage asked.

Adam shook his head.

"Your father is happy for the first time in months. Logan is a good man and a close friend. I just don't want to see anyone hurt." Gage looked sincere as he spoke.

"Don't worry, Gage. I screwed up, but I'll fix it. My reaction actually has nothing to do with their relationship."

Gage nodded and looked back toward the house. "You want to talk about it?"

Did he? Gage was a wonderful Alpha and Adam really could use his advice. "If you don't mind."

"Of course not." Gage waved him toward to a couple of benches located close by. Adam followed him over and took a seat where he could see the back door where Tasha was entering.

"She's a great woman and Marissa already loves Crystal," Gage said. "You're very lucky."

"I am," Adam agreed. He stared after Tasha even though she was no longer in sight.

"It's not easy starting a relationship when you're an Alpha," Gage said. "But I assure you, it's worth it."

Adam snapped his head back to his companion. Gage was smiling at him. "I'm having trouble believing that she really wants to be with me and doesn't feel obligated."

"Oh, she does," Gage said. "We can all see that."

"Really?"

Gage smiled. "Women are tricky creatures. Marissa had it in her head she was going to leave even after we became mates."

Adam looked up. He hadn't known that. "How'd you make her stay?"

Gage shook his head. "I didn't. She knew her place was with me. Her head and her heart just couldn't agree. At least Tasha seems dedicated to her family and you."

"Tasha and Crystal have already had a rough time of it. I'd hate to cause them any more pain."

"Who says you'll cause them pain?" the other Alpha asked thoughtfully. "Maybe it's you she's been waiting on to take the pain *away*. It's not easy taking care of people.

You're seeing that yourself. Imagine doing it all alone with no support."

Adam leaned back and paused. "I hadn't thought of it that way. Tasha is a great sister, though."

"She's smart and caring. Much like you," Gage said.

"Thank you," Adam said, a little embarrassed. "That compliment means a lot coming from you."

"You'll make a good Alpha. You're kind and caring but strong. All you have to do is believe in yourself." Gage met his gaze.

"I have some big shoes to fill," Adam admitted.

"Yes, I know. I've been there. And, like me, you already have a big supporter in your corner. Your father wouldn't have left the Pack to you if you weren't ready. Son or not."

"I want to believe that," Adam confessed. "But this happened with Logan and he didn't tell me."

"It's not easy when your entire life is changing," Gage said.

"Which is exactly what Tasha just told me. Instead of considering what Christian was going through, I panicked and hurt him. I was so worried about how I was doing as an Alpha."

Gage laughed. "You're going to make mistakes. More than you think you'll be making."

"Great, you make it sound like so much fun."

"It is," Gage assured him. "Every day will have trials and every day will have greatness."

"I can't wait to experience that," Adam said. He really meant it, too.

"I figure you'll be leaving soon?"

"Yes," Adam replied. "In the morning. I still have decisions to make."

"Putting together your inner circle? If you need anything, please let me know," Gage offered.

"Thank you."

"But I think you need to have one more conversation tonight," Gage said. Adam followed Gage's gaze.

His father and Logan had just stepped out onto the deck. Christian looked uneasy. Logan immediately slung an arm around Christian's shoulder to show support. That simple action proved the two men had more than just a sexual bond. Adam liked seeing that Logan would publicly comfort Christian.

"Logan won't leave your Pack," Adam whispered as the realization hit him.

"No, he won't. I'm sorry, Adam."

Christian said something to Logan, then began the short walk to him.

"I'll give the two of you some privacy," Gage said before he patted Adam's shoulder.

Adam couldn't believe how nervous he was. This was his dad, the man who'd raised him. At one time Adam would have told his father everything. He stood, waiting for Christian to reach him.

"Join me?" Adam waved to the bench that Gage had just vacated.

"Thank you," Christian said, rubbing his hands together.

This was a lot harder than Adam could have imagined. There were a thousand things that he wanted to say, but he couldn't seem to make himself speak. The lines of stress plain under Christian's eyes were because of him. He felt terrible.

"Adam."

"No!" He almost yelled.

Christian flinched.

"Shit." Adam rubbed his hands roughly over his face. "First, I apologize for the outburst earlier. I was taken by surprise, but I didn't mean any disrespect toward you or Logan," Adam started. "It didn't even have anything to do with you or Logan. I'm an idiot and all this stress has been getting to me. I panicked and know that even if you don't love me —"

"What?" Christian blinked at him and shook his head. "Adam, slow down. You're not making any sense."

Adam couldn't sit still, so he rose and began to pace. "I shouldn't have run off that way. I acted like a child."

His father sighed. "I've wanted to tell you so many times. I didn't want you to find out like this. I can understand why you reacted the way you did."

"Why *didn't* you tell me? Why keep this a secret?" That was the question that kept circling in his mind. "Are you embarrassed of Logan or me?"

"No," Christian said quickly. "You were so young when your mother died. I know you don't remember much about her."

"My mom?" Adam didn't understand what his mom had to do with anything. He started to ask, but his father held up his hand.

"Just let me get through this."

Adam nodded, so Christian continued, "I met Logan a couple of years before your mom. We connected immediately. But when my father made a deal with the Alpha of the Pack to mate me with his daughter, I had to give him up," Christian explained.

"You were with Logan before Mom?" Adam couldn't help but interrupt.

"Yes. It was hard, but I finally came out to my father. He took it much better than I could have ever hoped. When I told my father that I loved Logan, he had already made the deal. He felt bad, but there was nothing he could do. He would have lost the Pack if he'd broken the arrangement."

Adam opened, then closed his mouth. His mind raced. In truth, he hadn't thought of his mom in so long. When he'd seen his father with Logan, he still hadn't thought of her. "There had to be something you could have done."

"Things were different back then. Two men didn't openly date or even think about going public with a relationship with another. And I did need a wife to give the Pack pups."

"Did you see Logan when you were mated to my mom?" He had to know.

"No." Christian shook his head fiercely. "Logan left the

Pack and joined this one. I told your mother the truth right after we were mated and she seemed okay with it. Even asked if I wanted to see him." Christian laughed. "Your mother was wonderful. She never made me feel bad about my feelings for Logan. After we'd been together for ten years, she went behind my back and contacted him."

Adam gasped in astonishment.

"Yes. I was quite shocked myself. She knew that I loved her, but, without Logan, I was incomplete."

"What happened?" Adam's voice was just above a whisper. He had so many questions. He'd always heard how his mother had put everyone above herself. She had been one of the most unselfish and caring persons anyone had known. Stories from his dad and others in the Pack were all he really had of the woman who'd given birth to him, but they had always made him feel closer to her.

"Well...Logan came to visit." Christian's eyes clouded as if he were revisiting a memory. Adam found himself scooting closer, wanting to share it. "At first, I was so mad at her I could have strangled her. But then she calmly told both of us that we either needed to get over each other or admit our feelings out loud and in front of her." Christian met his gaze. "So we did. And do you know what your mother did?"

Adam shook his head. There was no telling.

"She kissed me."

Adam only frowned. What could he say to that? "And?"

Christian laughed deeper than. "She asked Logan if he wanted to kiss me."

"He did." Adam knew somehow.

His father smiled. "He did. When we finally broke apart, we turned to your mother and her smile was as big as the state."

"She was happy about it?"

"After we kissed, she walked up just as bold as can be and kissed Logan."

Adam jolted. "What?"

"It seems after years of me talking about Logan, then getting to know him herself, she had gained feelings for him, too."

It was too much. Adam jumped onto his feet and backed away. "Are you telling me that the three of you...?"

His father nodded. "Until she died."

"I don't think I want to hear anymore." Adam put his hand on his stomach and turned away. It wasn't as though he was new to the world of ménage. He'd even participated in a few. But they were talking about his mother here. "Why did you tell me this?"

"Because I wanted you to understand I am not betraying your mother. I loved her very much. And she loved both Logan and me." Christian stood and stepped closer so he could grasp Adam's shoulder. "As Alpha of the Pack, I had to hide my feelings for him. I won't hide them any longer."

"You shouldn't have to," Adam said. "I would never ask you to. But that doesn't explain why you didn't tell me at least."

"I wanted to give you time to adjust to your position. You've been worried sick about me," Christian said.

"I have."

"I'm sorry, Adam," Christian said. "I have been going crazy with guilt keeping this from you."

Hysterical laughter escaped until Adam thought he'd fall over. "I thought you wanted to end your existence!"

"No, son. This is such a mess. I just didn't want to see disgust in your eyes when you look at me. I love you and I couldn't take that," Christian admitted emotionally. His father's eyes teared up.

"I just want you to be happy. I don't care if it's with Logan or half the men in the Pack."

His father embraced him. "Don't let Logan hear you say that."

Adam slapped his dad on the back. "You got it."

"We should have talked about this earlier," Christian said. "All of this confusion would have been avoided."

"Yeah," Adam agreed. "But it wouldn't have been as much fun."

Christian laughed. "You'll come back soon?"

"Of course," Adam said. "We're actually letting Crystal stay here for a couple of weeks. We'll be back to pick her up."

"And Logan and I will come see you."

Adam glanced up and saw Logan was still on the porch, wringing his hands. "Maybe we should let him come join us. He looks like he's about to have a fit."

"He's scared that he's going to come between us. Or you hate him. Or —"

"I get it." Adam waved off his father. "Logan!" he yelled and gestured. "Come here."

Logan jumped and, even from where Adam stood with his father, he could see that the older man blushing.

"Ah, that's so cute," Adam teased.

"Oh, shut up." Christian hugged him, though.

Adam leaned his head on his father's shoulder, happy and content.

Chapter Six

Adam poured two glasses full of whiskey before he turned around and handed one to his guest. He'd only been home twenty-four hours, but he'd been busy. No more excuses — he was going to have his inner circle in place within the next few weeks and it would all start with his new Enforcer.

"Thank you for coming," Adam said.

"I'll be honest, even after I'd sent you the email, I didn't think I'd hear back from you."

He shook his head. "I can't think of a better Enforcer."

Larry laughed. "Sure, after you pay off your Pack."

"You saved my best friend's girl and you ended the terror that was affecting all the Packs," Adam pointed out. "You were the second in command for Riker's Pack."

Larry frowned. "That's not exactly an accomplishment. You've heard the stories about how Riker ran his Pack."

"I have," Adam agreed. "But after I got your email, I started to talk to the other shifters inside Riker's Pack, including the ones who had left."

"You did?"

"Yes," Adam replied with a smile. "So, I heard about how you protected the others in the Pack from Riker's temper. Took the punishments onto yourself."

"I don't know what you're talking about," Larry lied.

"Of course," Adam said. He hadn't expected any other answer. "Also, several of your old Pack members told me that even when they weren't coming to you for anything, you took care of everything. You made the decisions."

Larry shrugged. "I did my job. That doesn't mean anyone here will accept me. As much as I want to belong to a Pack again, I do have to warn you that I will not be a popular choice. Even your best friend hates me."

Adam had thought about all of this. He'd spoken to the Council, Gage, Lamont, his father and Tony. The only person he hadn't asked advice from was Cain, because Larry was right on that front. Even though Larry had in fact saved Emily from Brent, the shifter who'd been behind the attacks on the Packs' females, Cain still didn't trust Larry.

Instead of telling anyone what he'd suspected, Larry had followed Brent.

Larry had gotten there in time before Brent hurt Emily. Cain still believed that had Larry told them, Emily would have never been put in danger in the first place.

Both men were right.

Adam could clearly see why Larry had done what he did. But he also understood Cain's point of view.

However, what was best for his Pack was having a strong, loyal and confident second in command. A shifter who could take on the roles of both the Beta and Enforcer. That was going to be Larry. Adam didn't care who he'd have to convince. Every other Alpha had agreed and so had the Council. Plus, if the Council went ahead with announcing their presence to the world, then Adam was really going to need someone to help protect the Pack.

"Let me take care of Cain and anyone else," Adam said. "Your concern will be to strengthen the security around here and bonding with the Pack."

Larry nodded. "I can take care of our safety, no problem. The latter might be more difficult."

"No," Adam said. "I'm bringing back the full-moon runs and weekly gatherings. When the weather is nice, we'll have it here in the back. During winter or if it rains, we have the community center."

Larry looked thoughtful. Adam leaned forward and placed his hand on Larry's arm. "What?"

"It's been a long time since I've felt a sense of Pack. Even when I was with Riker, we only got together when he wanted a battle or fight."

Adam shook his head, saddened by Larry's life.

"But I remember when I was younger and still in my birth Pack," Larry continued. "Every Sunday we would go to the Alpha house and eat and play. There were always games for the younger kids and the teenagers would shift and run. I loved it."

"That's what I want to bring back," Adam said. "The pride in the Pack. We've been through so much with the attack on Mindy, then a new Alpha."

"It's a good idea," Larry stated. "This is the kind of Pack that I want to belong to."

This was working out perfectly. Not only would he get someone he could trust, but Larry could connect with his kind again. It wasn't easy being Rogue. Adam didn't actually know anyone who didn't belong to a Pack, but he'd heard his father and other Alphas talk about how dangerous rogue shifters could become.

A shifter, or at least a wolf shifter, needed the Pack to keep them calm and to hold on to their humanity. The nature of the wolf was to belong, to lead or follow, and while shifters were human, they also had some wolf instincts. Adam couldn't imagine what it was like for Larry not to belong with anyone or in a territory. He could guess that it was better than living under Riker's rule, though.

Riker, an Alpha from one of the Colorado Packs, ran his Pack with fear and discipline. Anyone in the higher position had fought for them. That was how Larry had become Riker's second in command. He'd beaten all others for the position. Everyone knew that Riker only accepted the strongest and meanest into the fold, so that reputation was going to make it tough to bring in Larry. But Adam had faith in his Pack.

"So what do you say?" Adam asked. "Will you be my second?"

Larry sipped his whiskey. "I really want to say yes."

Relief flooded Adam.

"But I don't know if I can."

"Why not?" Adam pressed. "If it's what you want."

"We both know it'll need some time for me to be accepted. You're taking a chance of your Pack turning on you," Larry told him.

"They wouldn't," Adam promised. He believed in his Pack one hundred percent.

"Maybe we should take this slow and see what kind of reception I get?" Larry sounded really concerned.

Adam didn't know how to assure him that he was going to find a home with them. He studied Larry and saw that he nervously bounced his leg. Concentrating, Adam pulled in Larry's scent. Not only was Larry giving off nervous tics, but he smelled almost desperate. It hit him.

"I won't turn my back on you," Adam said quietly.

Larry jerked up his head.

"Do you think that if this doesn't work out, I'll send you away?" Adam asked.

"This isn't the first time I've approached an Alpha or had one come to me," Larry told him. "At first, everyone seems to accept me, but when out of the Alpha's sight, they gang up on me, trying to push me into some sort of conflict."

Damn, Adam'd had no idea. He moved from the couch to sit on the coffee table right in front of Larry. Now, he determined even more to add Larry to his Pack.

"Look at me," Adam demanded.

Larry complied and Adam could see the wariness in his gaze.

"I can't promise you that you'll be accepted on the first day. We both know how hard this is going to be. I will guarantee you that you will belong to this Pack, to me, until you chose to leave."

"Right." Larry nodded, but it was obvious he still didn't believe Adam.

"I don't know how the other Alphas worked, but I want you to be my second. If anything happens to me, you'll take over until another Alpha is in place or you take the position. But you will have the support of the entire Pack, including the inner circle. One that you're going to help me put in place."

"You want me to pick your inner circle?" Larry questioned cautiously.

"*Our* inner circle," Adam corrected.

"This sounds too good to be true," Larry told him.

Adam nodded. "What if you stayed a few days and got to know the people inside the house? If there are any issues, we'll take care of them jointly and see how we work together. Can you give me forty-eight hours?"

Larry leaned forward to brace his elbows on his knees. "That sounds fair."

Adam smiled. "That will give us time to work on Pack business. We won't announce your position until you tell me you're ready."

"Deal." Larry held out his hand and Adam quickly accepted. He'd be relying on his Pack to make Larry feel welcome.

"Great." Adam clapped his hands together. "My sister should have dinner ready. Tonight, it'll just be a few of us. And that's a good place to start."

"Okay." Larry stood and wiped his hands on his slacks in a nervous gesture.

If anyone had asked Adam if he'd have thought Larry would be anxious about a simple dinner, Adam would have laughed. Larry might have been one of the scariest shifters around, but Adam knew he still felt unease and the need to fit in. It was actually quite sweet.

Adam rose and motioned to the door before turning to lead the way. When he stepped into the hall, he spotted one of their younger guards. Hector had been the first who'd come to Adam, asking if he could apply for a position becoming available. Adam had decided that no one would fight for a place in his Pack. They could apply and be accepted or not, based on their skills. If they wanted to work on certain techniques, he'd be talking to Lamont,

Cain's father and Alpha, on some additional training. He wanted every member of his Pack to feel as though they could accomplish their dreams. Adam was there to help.

Hector nodded to first him, then Larry. Adam smiled in response. Hector knew who Larry was, since he'd been the one to let Larry in and Adam had introduced them.

Larry tilted his head back at Hector as Adam stopped in front of the young guard.

"We're headed to dinner," Adam said. "You're about off shift. Would you like to join us?"

"Yes, sure." Hector nearly bounced on the toes of his feet. "That would be great." He glanced over at Larry. "Maybe later I can ask you for a few tips?"

"Tips?" Larry repeated.

"I'm new, not to the Pack, but as a guard. Adam is letting me work inside for now, but I really want to get out and do more. Perhaps…maybe…I could use some advice."

Larry smiled and it brightened his entire face. "I would be honored."

"Really?" Hector shrieked.

"Sure, man." Larry slapped him on the back. "After dinner, we'll head out back and I'll show you a few moves." Larry turned to Adam. "I'm going to wash up real quick."

"Last door on the right," Adam told him.

Hector made it until Larry closed the door behind him before he grabbed Adam's arm and shook him.

"Calm down," Adam told him, laughing.

"I'm so excited. Everyone says that next to Cain, Larry is the best fighter. I can't believe he's going to show me some moves!"

Yeah, Larry was going to make it just fine. Adam grasped the back of Hector's neck playfully and pushed him down the hall. "We'd better get to the kitchen before Laura comes looking for us."

Hector babbled the entire time they strolled down the long hall toward the swinging doors leading into the kitchen. Adam loved the dark wood floor and matching paneling, but maybe it was time for a change. They could brighten up the path from the front door to the kitchen. His dad had always talked about making changes from the time he took over, but had never actually done so. Adam could and he would.

Laura was humming when they pushed through the door into the kitchen. The smell of roast filled the air and his mouth immediately started to water. He'd only been gone a few days, but he'd missed his sister's cooking. She ran a small catering company in town, but it was the homemade meals she cooked for family that meant so much.

"Hi." She glanced around. "Oh, isn't Larry staying, too?"

"I'm right here, ma'am," Larry said as he entered. "I've been smelling your dinner all night."

Laura giggled. Holy shit, his sister actually giggled.

Adam had told Laura all about his decision regarding Larry and she'd been supportive. She knew the story of how Larry had saved Emily and automatically agreed that Larry would be a great addition to the Pack. Laura was also aware of the Council business about taking the shifters public. But Adam had never seen her blush and giggle like she was now.

"Can I help set the table?" Larry offered.

"Already done," Laura replied shyly. "But you can take this there." She handed Larry a large bowl of potatoes and carrots.

"Yes, ma'am." Larry smiled and did as he'd been charged. Hector followed along, asking Larry questions.

Adam sidled up to his sister. "Larry's very handsome, don't you think?"

"What?" Laura fumbled with a stirring spoon. Adam laughed. "Oh, shut up." Laura hip-bumped him. "I just didn't expect him to be so...big."

"Uh-huh." Adam was really enjoying this. There had been so much stress lately that he and Laura hadn't gotten to play and tease. It felt good. Another puzzle piece falling into place.

"So where's Tasha?" Laura asked. "I'm surprised you could peel yourself away from her for dinner."

Adam waved his finger in Laura's face. "Nice attempt at changing the subject." He picked up the large plate of homemade rolls. "And she's on her way."

He strolled toward the table, letting his sister off the hook, for now. "Who else is joining us?" he asked.

"Mable and James," Laura said.

That was good. James was the head guard and Larry would have to work closely with him. James had been given the position five years ago. But since he was one of the younger shifters that worked for his father, Adam planned on keeping him. Mabel was the accountant for the Pack. Several of the members worked in businesses located in town that the Alpha financed. First his grandfather, then his dad and now him. Adam hoped they'd be able to expand even more. He knew a couple of people in his Pack who wanted to open a few small businesses. The plan was to schedule three openings in the next twelve months. It would bring revenue into the Pack while allowing his members to do what they loved. Mabel was only doing the Alpha's books at the moment, but Adam wanted to talk to her about playing a bigger role. Bringing both her and James into the inner circle would be the second step.

A knock on the sliding glass door caught his attention. He looked over and saw Tasha standing outside. Hector was closest, so he opened the door and waved Tasha in. Adam set the rolls on the table before moving to her. He didn't care who was in the room. He yanked Tasha close and kissed her deeply. She didn't show any hesitation, wrapping her arms around his neck and kissing him back.

Someone cleared their throat and Adam pulled back to see James and Mabel behind Tasha. Adam had been so fixated on her he hadn't seen the other two shifters.

"Evening, boss," James said as he passed them.

Adam nodded to him, then Mabel. "Glad you could both join us."

"As if we'd miss Laura's roast," James said, prior to kissing Laura on the cheek. She swatted him but laughed. The look was completely different from when she'd been flirting with Larry. Adam wondered if there was a real connection between his sister and his new Enforcer.

"What's going on?" Tasha whispered.

"I'll tell you later," Adam murmured in her ear. "Let's sit down and eat. I can't wait to get you back in my bed."

She laughed before slipping out from his hold.

Adam glanced over and saw Larry shaking hands with James, then Mabel. Adam could see that Larry was nervous again, but James was being his usual lighthearted self and was already joking with Larry. Laura finished bringing the rest of the food to the table.

"Time to eat," she announced.

Adam took the seat at the head of the table with Tasha on his left. Laura guided Larry to the chair to Adam's right before sitting beside him. Hector, James and Mabel filled in the rest of the empty seats. Adam looked around at the people joining him. He hoped this would be the first of many dinners with his Pack. He reached over and covered Tasha's hand, giving her a squeeze before smiling at the others. "Let's eat!" They didn't need a speech from him. Just time to enjoy one another's company.

Laura began passing the platter of roast around. Adam filled his plate. He hoped to burn off the calories later with Tasha.

* * * *

Tasha followed Adam up the stairs toward the bedroom, keeping her hand in his. The evening had been fun and full of good conversation.

At one point Larry and James had taken Hector out into the back lawn and worked out with him, showing him different moves and tricks. Adam, her, Laura and Mabel had sat on the porch drinking coffee and discussing the future of the Pack. Mabel had been excited about the opportunity that Adam offered.

Tasha could feel the bonds of the Pack forming around Adam. She knew they existed, but even with Christian she hadn't actually been aware of it happening. This was a new experience for her — for most of the Pack. Most everyone had been born under Christian or his dad's reign. The ones under Christian's father remembered when Christian had taken over, but most of them were no longer around. Christian's Pack was becoming Adam's and over thirty members were feeling the change.

"You okay?" Adam asked when they reached his bedroom.

Tasha turned in his arms. "I am perfect."

"Yes, you are." Adam lowered his head and brushed his lips over hers.

"More," Tasha demanded when Adam tried to pull back.

He lifted her so she had no choice but to wrap her legs around his waist. Tasha's back hit the closed door as Adam began to rut against her. She clawed at his shirt, trying to get the fabric out of the way. She wanted to be skin to skin.

He ripped his mouth from hers. "This would be more comfortable in bed."

Tasha laughed. "Yeah? So take me to bed."

Adam tightened his hold under her ass and hitched her up before he turned the door knob and they almost fell though the opening. Tasha clung to him to keep her balance.

"Hang on tight," Adam ordered, slamming the door behind them.

As if she needed to be told. He carried her across the room, but instead of falling onto the mattress as she expected, Adam gently laid her down. Tasha watched him as he stepped back. "What are you doing?" she asked.

He grinned. "Stay there."

"What if I don't?" she teased, giving him her best pout.

"If you do what I say, you'll really enjoy it," he promised.

Tasha grinned this time.

Adam took several steps backward before he spun around and ran to the bathroom. The water in the tub turned on and she frowned. What was he doing? She'd thought that they were going to bed. She started to sit up.

"Stay where you are!"

Tasha dropped back down onto the mattress. There was no way that Adam could have seen her, but he'd somehow known her curiosity was getting the better of her. "If you don't hurry up, I'll start without you!" she called.

"Go ahead."

That was not the answer she'd expected. Oh, well, if he wanted to tease her, then Tasha would have to hurry him along. She squirmed out of her clothes but made sure that she stayed on the bed. He'd only told her to stay where she was. He hadn't said she couldn't move at all.

Once she was naked, Tasha started to knead her breasts. Adam seemed to approve of them, as the evidence of the small marks made by his sucking told. Tasha laid her head back and moaned as she played with herself.

Keeping one hand where it was, she trailed the other down her stomach to her pussy. She ran her fingers through her slick folds before letting one tip tease her entrance.

Tasha closed her eyes, no longer worrying about Adam.

It felt amazing, sliding her finger into her pussy. She pumped the digit in and out before adding another. Lifting her hips off the mattress, Tasha managed to lose herself in the pleasure.

"I thought I told you not to move?" Adam said, running his hand up her leg.

"Did you?" Tasha asked, looking up at him.

Adam grinned. "Here, let me help you."

"Oh, now you want to help?" Tasha taunted. She spread her thighs wider so that he'd have an even better view.

He growled before pulling her hand away.

"Ah," she whined.

"Come here." He picked her up off the bed.

"What are we doing?"

"Taking a bath," Adam said.

"A bath?" Tasha echoed.

"A nice, long hot bath," Adam said.

"Together?"

He didn't respond as he carried her into the bathroom. Adam had filled the large whirlpool-style tub with water and had even added bubbles. Several candles were lit along a shelf across the room. Adam hit the switch to turn off the lights.

"This is so romantic," she whispered. Tasha hadn't expected all of this. All she'd wanted was to spend a little time with Adam before sleeping in his arms. Tasha was glad Adam had invited her over. She didn't want to ever spend another night without him. It was too soon for them to commit in that way, but Tasha wasn't going to worry.

"It's a good thing you've already got undressed," Adam said. He bent and tested the water with his hand before lowering her in.

She couldn't hold back a moan of delight as the hot water flowed over her. It was the absolute perfect temperature. Once she was fully emerged, Adam stepped back, then started to undress. Tasha watched him slowly expose every inch of his fantastic body. The candlelight gave her just enough brightness to see him without having to use her shifter eyesight.

"You're gorgeous," she murmured.

Adam grinned before he pulled off his final piece of clothing. His entire body was hard but especially his cock.

Tasha slid over and motioned him closer. "Come join me," she pleaded.

"I am," he told her. Adam dipped his toe in the water before climbing in behind her.

Tasha leaned back against his strong chest. "This is nice."

"It is," he agreed. Adam cupped a handful of bubbles, then spread them over her breasts. Yeah, she knew his favorite parts of her body. "So soft."

"Hmm," Tasha hummed. She moved her legs under the

water as he slid his other hand down. "Touch me."

"Yes," he whispered while dragging his fingers over her clit, before he plunged two in deep.

She arched in pleasure.

"That's it," he encouraged.

Tasha lifted so that each time he thrust his fingers, she was getting them as deep as possible. With his free hand, he plucked at one nipple. "Adam."

"Yes," he hissed, pumping his cock up against her lower back.

She reached behind with one arm while tilting her head so that she could bring his mouth to hers. Tasha sucked on his tongue until he was bucking quickly against her. She tore her mouth away.

"Inside me," she panted.

"Lift up for me."

Tasha braced her palms at the bottom of the tub while raising her ass. Adam gripped her hips and pulled her back until she hovered over his erection.

"Come down slowly."

His hand brushed her pussy as he held himself. Once she felt the tip of his cock inside her, she carefully began to lower herself.

"Oh, God," she whispered.

"You're so tight," Adam said. "Hurry."

Tasha dropped her head back onto his shoulder as she finished taking him in. Adam cupped her breasts and pulled at her nipples.

"Ride me."

She loved the huskiness in his voice. "Hang on," she warned. Tasha pulled her legs back until she was on her knees. "I'm going to take what I want."

"Go for it."

Tasha closed her eyes as she started rocking her hips. Lowering herself up and down while adding a small circle gave her the perfect amount of friction. It didn't hurt that Adam kept manipulating her nipple with one hand and her clit with the other. Water came dangerously close to splashing over the rim of the tub, but she didn't care. She doubted that Adam did, either, by the way he was panting against her neck.

This time might not be as hot or passionate as the other, but Tasha loved the soft and sweet rhythm of their lovemaking. She was all for hard and fast, but sometimes she wanted to be romanced and Adam had more than given her that.

The bubbly water, fragrant candles and gentle coupling were perfect.

As her body began to tremble, she knew her climax was building. Her clit tingled and her toes curled. "Oh," she moaned low.

"That's it, baby," Adam encouraged.

Tasha kept riding him until she was completely spent. She sank down against him.

Adam was still pumping his hips.

"What do you need?" she asked. She wasn't a selfish lover, even when she was absolutely exhausted.

"Just stay still," he said.

"Okay," she agreed.

Adam was doing all the work now. He held her legs up and open so he could thrust inside.

"Almost there," he murmured.

Tasha grasped the sides of the tub. "Harder."

Adam kept plunging, until he groaned and came. Tasha grinned. "Perfect."

He wrapped his arms around her and she settled back with his cock still half-hard. "Oh, don't worry," she whispered. "I still have enough for another round once I get us into bed."

"Hmm."

That sounded good to her.

Chapter Seven

"Good morning!"

Adam grunted at the loud voice interrupting his peaceful sleep. Beside him, Tasha groaned.

"Rise and shine!"

This had to be a joke, a really sick joke. Adam lifted his head and peered at Cain from where he stood at the end of Adam's bed.

"Seriously, Cain," he grumbled.

"I was just in the neighborhood," Cain said, dropping down on the side of the bed.

"Right." Adam wasn't buying that.

"Make him go away," Tasha mumbled.

Adam smiled before he noticed that half of Tasha's body was in full view. He growled before yanking the blanket over her.

"Oh, come now," Cain said. "I wasn't even looking. Emily would scratch my eyes out."

"Yes, she would," Adam replied. "And if you don't leave us alone, I'm going to tell her."

"It's not my fault the two of you weren't properly clothed when I arrived."

Adam shook his head, but sat up. "What are you doing here?"

"Funny story," Cain said, but the look on his face held worry not amusement. "I'd just gotten to my dad's last night when I overheard him telling Tony that you've picked your Enforcer."

Well, shit, Adam had wanted to be the one to tell him. "Cain—"

"I knew something must be wrong," Cain said. "There is no way that you're going to trust that guy."

"I do," Adam told him. "This is what we need."

"What are you thinking?" Cain shouted.

Tasha popped up. "No." She pointed at Cain. "You listen to Adam and let him explain. He needs your support."

Cain frowned.

"You are his best friend, aren't you?" she asked, with a raised eyebrow.

"Yes," Cain hissed. "Damn it."

Adam couldn't help but grin. Tasha was a force and she wasn't going to allow anyone, not even his best friend, to give him shit.

"Now go downstairs to talk about this. Someone kept me up half the night," Tasha said before plopping back down, then yanking the blankets over her head.

"Go start the coffee," Adam told Cain.

His best friend nodded before rising, then walking out. Adam turned back to Tasha and pulled the blanket off her face. "Thank you."

She opened his eyes while smiling. "You're welcome. You've got to stand by your decision. I like Larry and he needs a Pack."

"I agree," Adam said. "He won't be going anywhere and I know Cain will come around."

"Give me a kiss." She lifted her head to accept it as he lowered his head.

Adam swept his tongue inside her mouth, needing a taste of her. He pulled back, then brushed the hair off her forehead. She was absolutely the most beautiful person he'd ever seen. "Get some more sleep."

"Okay."

Adam was more than amused when she rolled over. It was true that he'd kept her up late. He felt pretty damn good about that. He just couldn't get enough of her. But he couldn't bask this morning, since his best friend had decided to show up. He groaned when he rolled out of bed. A pair of jeans lay over a chair, so he grabbed them and slipped them on before heading toward the door. He grabbed his cell phone off the dresser as he passed and shoved it into his back pocket.

He took one last look at Tasha bundled up in the blankets before exiting the room. It was a good thing that his body temperature ran hot, since there was a definite chill to the air. Adam rubbed his arms but didn't want to go back to his room and risk waking Tasha again.

It was early so he didn't hear anyone else moving around. Except for the big pissed-off shifter in the kitchen. Adam padded down the stairs, running what he wanted to say through his mind. It was important that Cain backed him up here and Adam knew that his best friend would eventually see things his way.

Adam pushed through the swinging door of the kitchen and spotted Cain sitting at the island staring into a mug of coffee. He strolled over to the coffeemaker, then poured a cup.

"Talk," Cain demanded.

Adam leaned against the counter across from him and sipped. Cain needed to calm down before they could have a rational conversation. He didn't smell Emily in the house, so Cain had come alone. That wasn't going to help. At least Emily could make Cain listen most of the time. It appeared Adam was on his own.

"Fine!" Cain held up his hands. "Can you tell me what you were thinking inviting that man into your Pack? As your Enforcer?"

"That man," Adam said calmly, "saved your mate."

Cain snorted. "If he'd told us what he suspected, Emily wouldn't have been in danger in the first place."

"Cain." Adam was tired of this same argument. "We don't know that. If he'd told us, there would have been questions. Brent would have gotten a head start and he might have actually killed Emily. Larry didn't know that Brent was headed to your Pack. He only suspected that Brent was responsible."

"He could have called once he got close," Cain argued. "Tony could have gotten her away."

"Tony and Emily were in their wolf form," Adam reminded him.

Cain slammed his hand on the counter. "She could have died."

Adam set his mug behind him before pushing away from the counter. He reached out and covered Cain's palm with his, offering his friend comfort. "You can't go on blaming Larry for what could have happened. The important thing is nothing *did* happen to Emily. You have to let this go."

"I know," Cain said softly. "But when it comes to Emily, I can't think rationally."

"If it's any consolation, I would do things differently if I could."

Adam and Cain both jumped.

Larry stood just inside the doorway. "I know you're angry at me, but I did do what I thought was best at the time."

"Cain," Adam warned as his best friend stood slowly. He did not want a confrontation in the middle of his kitchen.

"She still has nightmares," Cain whispered. "Even running anywhere near the spot where Brent went after her causes her to lose control."

"If I could have put it together sooner, I might have been able to stop Brent from leaving. Or talked to you guys. He'd already taken off when I realized something wasn't right about him."

"Cain." Adam stepped up behind his friend and clasped Cain's shoulder. "It's not his fault."

Larry stepped forward. "I made a mistake, but Adam is giving me another chance and I really want to be a part of his Pack. I want a home for once in my life."

If anyone could understand second chances, it had to be Cain. He'd screwed things up with Emily so badly when they were younger no one thought that she'd ever forgive him. She had, giving Cain a second chance, and they'd found love together.

"You have to protect Adam," Cain said. "He's my best friend. You can't be an Enforcer if you don't trust the people around you."

Larry nodded. "I know. And I'm trying."

Cain nodded, then turned to Adam. "He's a good choice."

"I know." Adam was so damn relieved.

"So…" Cain rubbed his hands together. "How're you going to do this?"

Adam laughed. "You two sit down and I'll make us some breakfast while we talk."

"Sure," Cain said, then surprised both Adam and Larry when he threw his arm around Larry's neck and towed him toward the island. Cain pushed Larry onto one of the stools before sitting beside him. "Make us breakfast, Alpha."

"Eggs and bacon?" Adam asked as he headed toward the fridge. "While I'm doing this, we need to catch Larry up on what the Council is doing."

"The Alpha Council?" Larry asked. "What do they have to with anything?"

Adam waved his hand toward Cain to take over the conversation.

Cain sighed. "I barely understand this shit and you want me to explain it to someone else?"

"Your brother is involved," Adam pointed out.

"Make him explain," Cain countered.

Adam turned and glared. "Is Tony here right now? No! Because he doesn't break into people's houses at the ass crack of dawn and wake them up."

"So!" Cain turned to Larry. "How would you feel about all the shifters announcing themselves to the world?"

"What?" Larry exclaimed. "That's a terrible idea."

Cain chuckled. "Yeah, that was my first response, too."

"Keep explaining," Adam ordered as he started cooking.

"The number of shifters who have been killed because of hunting has doubled in recent years. Even with stiffer penalties for illegal hunting, it's not doing any good. We've had entire Packs wiped out."

"Jesus," Larry muttered. "I never thought about that."

"We've always managed to hide ourselves away from humans. We've lost a lot of shifters, of every species, because of it and now the Council is working with representatives of the other species for a solution," Cain said.

Adam didn't know why Cain had been reluctant to talk about it. He was actually explaining quite well.

"The best solution is announcing that shifters really do exist. Hope that by some of us coming forward, we can protect those of us left," Cain said.

"Some of us?" Larry asked.

"It won't be mandatory that any Pack goes public," Cain said. "That was decided very early on."

"A Pack will get to decide whether or not they want to be involved. If they want to remain in secret, we'll all continue to hide them," Adam shared. He plated the food before carrying two over to Cain and Larry.

"What are you, we, going to do?" Larry asked.

"I don't know," Adam confessed. "It's something that will be discussed with the inner circle, then decided."

"Speaking of the inner circle," Cain said. "Have you decided how many you'll chose?"

Adam grinned. "I bet it's driving you crazy not knowing."

"Just tell me!" Cain demanded.

Adam grabbed his own dish and set it down on the island so he was standing across from Cain and Larry. He took a large bite of eggs.

Cain growled.

Larry laughed.

"I hate you both," Cain complained.

"No, you don't," Adam said with a grin. "So far it's me, Larry, Mable and James."

"Okay." Cain nodded before biting off a piece of bacon. "You need at least two more, but four more would be better."

"I want to wait until I introduce the Pack to Larry before

I decide on any of the others," Adam said.

It was quiet for several moments before Larry cleared his throat. "Because you don't know who will accept me and who won't."

Adam didn't know what to say to that, since it was exactly the reason.

"Hey, man" — Cain clasped Larry's shoulder — "we'll get them to come around."

"And I have a plan," Adam told them.

"What?" Cain and Larry asked at the same time.

"How long can you stay?" Adam asked Cain.

"As long as you need me," Cain replied. "Emily's got a few days off so she's staying with the Pack. She wants to get started on the remodel of the house."

"She doesn't need you for that?" Larry questioned.

Cain laughed. "Since she pushed me out the door this morning," he said, "I think she wants me gone. We kept arguing about different shades of the same fucking color."

"So now she gets to decide," Larry pointed out.

"Ah." Cain waved his hand. "She has better taste than I do, anyway."

"Why were you arguing in the first place?" Larry asked.

"Because I could." Cain grinned.

"I see how much trouble you're going to be." Larry shook his head. "The rumors about you are obviously true."

"I'm not crazy," Cain said. "My mama had me tested."

Adam snorted coffee at Cain's repeated line from a television show. Cain loved using that line.

"What's your plan?" Larry asked ignoring Cain.

"We're going to throw a party!" Adam exclaimed.

"What?" Larry frowned. "How does that help?"

"Everyone loves a party," Cain announced.

"But how is that going to help the Pack accept me?"

"All anyone knows about you is that you were Riker's second in command. And that you stopped Brent and the attacks." Adam leaned toward him. "We're going to show everyone who you are on the inside. The man who stood in front of his Pack and took Riker's abuse so they didn't have to. The shifter who is strong enough to protect them, no matter what the Council decides."

"I will," Larry said. "I swear I will protect the Pack with my life."

"That's how I know you're who we need," Adam said. "So...are you in?"

Larry glanced from Adam to Cain and back to Adam. "I'm in."

"Yes!" Adam pumped his fist in the air.

Cain was grinning. "So when are we going to have this party?"

"Tomorrow," Adam said. "We'll have a barbecue, music, games, all kinds of fun. When the sun sets, we'll go on a run. The full Pack."

"Brilliant!" Cain applauded. "Bring the Pack close together again. It's what they need while cementing Larry's position."

Adam nodded.

"Are you sure?" Larry rubbed his hand on his jeans. "I could meet them in smaller groups."

"By having a celebration, we're showing them that the Alpha has already accepted you. If we take it too slowly, the Pack will wonder why," Cain told him.

"I guess," Larry replied. "It's just a lot of people to meet at once."

"Hey, I'll be by your side," Adam promised.

"Me, too," Cain added.

Larry peered at Cain. "I don't know if that's a good thing or a punishment."

Adam was so happy and relieved that he ignored Cain flipping Larry off and finished his food. Larry had accepted quicker than Adam had thought he would, so already he was ahead. Now if he could get the rest of his Pack behind the idea, everything would work out perfectly.

A knock sounded on the back door and Adam glanced up. Hector stood on the other side and waved.

"That's my cue," Larry said as he rose. "I promised Hector I would run him through some more training. He really wants to learn."

Adam beamed. Hector was a good kid and was going to be a true a benefit to the Pack when he was a little more seasoned.

"Cool!" Cain clapped his hands together and stood. "I'll come with you. It was a long drive and I could use some exercise."

Larry peered over at Adam.

"It's fine, just don't let him near anything sharp."

"Sure, boss," Larry replied before heading to the door with Cain following behind.

Adam waited until they were gone and the door was closed behind him before he looked around the kitchen. He had a lot to do to get ready for the party tomorrow. He pulled a pad of paper and pen from a drawer. *Food.* Laura could get help from some of the Pack and handle that. He'd put her in charge there. *Music.* Some of the young men had a band and they liked to play for everyone. He'd ask them to provide the entertainment. *Games.* The children would need something to do while the adults visited. Mabel had two kids so hopefully she had some ideas. *Set Up.* He, Larry, Cain and Tasha could handle putting out the tables and chairs. *Security.* He'd put James and Hector in charge of making sure the get-together was safe for everyone to attend. They would double the guards around the Alpha house so the Pack could see he was serious about their safety.

Now he just needed to get the word out to everyone. They had a phone tree in place in case of Pack problems that came up. He would dig that out and put it back into operation.

Satisfied, Adam set down the pen before glancing out of the back door. Larry and Cain were hard at work, teaching Hector. He had at least an hour before they would be done. That gave him some time he could spend with Tasha.

Yeah, she deserved a much better wakeup call than what

Cain had provided. Adam would make sure she came downstairs with a smile on her face.

Adam strode out of the kitchen, heading toward the stairs when his cell rang. He sighed before reaching back into his pocket and yanking out the ringing device. He didn't recognize the number, but with as many calls as had been coming in lately, that wasn't unusual any longer.

"Hello?" Adam answered.

"Alpha White. This is Austin Winters. I'm the Alpha of the southwest Colorado territory."

"Yes, hello." Adam had heard all about Austin and the small Pack he led. Austin's territory boarded Riker's and he was taking in a lot of the shifters who were escaping Riker. When Larry had made his break with the Pack, Riker's entire world had started to crumble. Austin had opened his door to the scared shifters, but he'd also invited trouble when Riker had found out. Adam had even heard that the Council had sent some of their own guards to help Austin. "I hope you're okay."

Austin's warm laugh traveled over the line. "It's not been easy but with some help everyone is safe and settling in. Riker has disappeared. That's why I'm calling."

"About Riker?" Adam clarified.

"Word has gotten around that Riker's second in command, Larry, has joined your Pack."

"Yes," Adam confirmed. "He's mine. Larry's accepted the position of our Enforcer."

"Good," Austin said. "I'm glad he's ended up somewhere where he'll be appreciated. The shifters who have joined my Pack all speak very highly of him."

"He's a good man," Adam said. "He'll not only be appreciated, but he'll also find a home here, and family."

"I hope so," Austin replied. "But you should know that Riker is looking for him. From what my new members are telling me, Riker has been searching for Larry and, as soon as Riker finds him, he plans on killing him. Riker has lost everything. The Council have orders for his arrest. He will do anything he can to take Larry down with him."

"Shit!" This was not what his Pack needed.

"I spoke to the Council. They sent four guards to me. I asked two of them if they'd help Larry and they agreed. With your permission, I can have them leave right away."

"Hold on." Adam had stopped in the middle of the hallway, but this wasn't a conversation he wanted to have in the open. He hurried to his office door and threw it open before slamming it shut behind him. He flipped on the light, then jogged to his desk so he could sit. "Sorry, can you give me their names?"

"Kurt Moore and Clint Price."

"Wait." Adam recognized the names. "Aren't those the two guards who'd attended the meeting at Riker's when we were searching for Brent?"

"Yes. The Council thought since they'd met Riker and already knew his scent, it would make it easier to track him. They haven't had any luck, but they are smart and can help keep your Pack safe if Riker does come there."

"Send them," Adam said. "We'll take all the help we can get. I won't let Larry deal with this on his own. He's mine and we will protect him."

"Great." Austin sounded relieved. "I know you're a new Alpha, but I have to say that this conversation leads me to believe you'll be a great one. You barely know Larry."

Pride burst through Adam at another Alpha's compliment. He wasn't doing this for recognition, though. This would be for Larry. It was time that his Enforcer had someone who'd fight for him. "Thank you. That means a lot to me."

"I'll have Kurt and Clint leave right away. They should be there sometime late this evening."

They could do this. Adam would be able to keep not only Larry safe but everyone in his Pack. With the Council's help, no one would hurt anyone else who was his again. "I'll make sure everything is ready for their arrival."

"If you need anything else, just let me know," Austin said. "Anything."

He couldn't believe how much support he was getting. The Packs all around the country were really showing that they cared about one another. It made Adam think that no matter what the Council decided, they were all going to be all right. "Thank you, Alpha Winters. And if you're ever in the area, we'd love to host you and your mate."

"Not mated yet," Austin said. "But once I'm sure my Pack's okay, I might take you up on your offer. Take care now."

"You, too." Adam hit the End button on the phone screen before he dropped the cell onto the desk. He had to go and tell Larry what was happening. He was even happier that Cain was there and could assist also, but Larry was who he was worried about.

"Fuck!" Adam slammed down his fist. Just as things were working out, something had to screw it up. No, he wasn't going to let anything mess up his plans. Adam stood, picked up his phone, then headed off to find his Enforcer. There was no telling where Riker was and they needed to put together a plan. More guards and a twenty-four-hour watch.

As he walked down the hall, he heard noise in the kitchen. Shit, he'd left a mess for Laura and never even thought about cleaning it up. She was not going to be happy. Instead of going through the kitchen, he took the coward's way out and exited through the back door in the hall.

Cain, Larry and Hector were still working out, but Adam could hear the laughter and playfulness. God, he didn't want to interrupt them, but he had no choice.

Larry was the first one who spotted him. "Hey, Adam."

He tried to smile but knew he'd failed when Larry sprinted to him.

"What's wrong?" Larry asked.

Cain and Hector were by Larry's side instantly.

"It's okay," Adam said. He gripped his Enforcer's shoulder. "We need to talk."

"Something's happened," Larry said.

"Yes," Adam admitted. "And now we're going to deal with it. Together. You are part of this Pack."

"Okay," Larry agreed.

* * * *

"We have to cancel the party." Larry jumped to his feet. "I have to leave."

"No!" everyone shouted at him.

Tasha was relieved when Adam grabbed Larry's arm and stopped his movements. She, Adam, Larry, Laura, Cain, James, Hector and Mabel were all sitting in the study where Adam had just told them that Riker was looking for Larry. She could understand Larry's reaction, but he wouldn't be safe on his own. He needed to stay with the Pack.

"I can't put everyone in danger," Larry stated.

"You aren't," Adam told him.

The disbelief on Larry's face was evident. "I haven't been a part of this Pack for twenty-four hours and already we have a crazy Alpha after us. You're bringing in guards from the Council."

"To keep you safe, to keep everyone safe," Adam said. "You're not leaving."

Larry turned and peered at the rest of them. Tasha had the feeling that he expected someone in the room to agree with him not Adam.

She stood. "Our Alpha is right. You are part of this Pack and we protect our own."

"You don't even know me," Larry ground out.

Tasha smiled. "Think about it this way. If anyone else in the room was going through what you are right now—had their old Alpha hunting them—would you send them off on their own?"

Larry shook his head.

"But you expect us to?" she pressed.

"It's...it's not the same thing."

God, whatever had happened to this poor shifter had

really messed with his head. She glanced at Adam to see if he wanted her to continue. She was hoping that since it wasn't Adam but a member of the Pack, Larry would realize they wanted him here. Adam gave her a small nod so she stepped forward, closer to Larry.

"Even if you weren't part of this Pack, we wouldn't let you face Riker alone," she told him.

"She's right," Cain added. "If you were just passing through town and stopped in our territory, we wouldn't let you leave without helping you."

Larry sighed. "I appreciate you all. I really do, but I feel so bad. I just don't want anyone hurt because of me."

"Just because you left doesn't mean Riker won't attack someone here, thinking you're either still here or to punish us for wanting you as part of this Pack," Tasha told him. "At least if you stick around you can help protect the Pack."

"Yeah, yes." Larry was nodding now. "But we should still cancel the barbecue tomorrow."

"We're not canceling," Adam stated firmly.

Tasha looked over at Adam. She actually agreed somewhat with Larry on this point.

"What?" he asked her.

She glanced around the room. Adam stepped closer and grasped her chin gently. "I want your honest opinion. It's important to me."

"I don't disagree," she told him. "We could postpone a couple of days."

"We don't even know if Riker is here yet," Adam said. "If we wait to have the party, he might actually be here. I think we should proceed, but with caution. We need to show the Pack that we'll stand together. We'll have every inch of the territory under guard."

"We'll also have help from the Council representatives," Cain added.

Larry sighed. "If they agree we should still have the get-together. I'll do it."

When Adam grinned, it made him look much younger and

even more handsome. Tasha loved seeing that expression on his face.

"Well," Laura said. "We should get started organizing."

"Is there anything I can do to help you?" Larry had turned to Laura.

Tasha couldn't miss the attraction that was sparking between Larry and Laura. Laura blushed slightly as she leaned toward Larry. She also had Larry's full attention.

"Not right now," Laura said quietly. "I need to make lists of what food we want and assign the dishes to some of the Pack."

"Well, if you need any help just let me know. I won't claim to be a great cook, but I can chop and stir," Larry offered.

"Okay." Laura giggled.

Tasha leaned against Adam when he slipped his arm around her waist. She peeped up at him and found Adam smiling over at Larry and Laura. It seemed she didn't need to ask Adam what he thought about the potential couple.

"Can I look at your guard roster?" Cain asked James.

"Sure." James stood. "I left my laptop in the car. I can go grab it."

"What can I do?" Hector questioned.

"Get every guard that is not currently on duty here," Adam stated. "I want to talk to them right now."

"I'll help Laura," Mabel said.

"Good." Adam turned to Tasha. "Can I see you for a minute in my office?"

"Sure," she agreed quickly. Tasha didn't know what he needed to say privately, but she hoped she could help.

He didn't release her hand as he drew her down the hall. Tasha didn't say anything until they were inside his office with the door closed.

"Are you okay?" she asked. "What can I do?"

"Come here." Adam lowered his head until his lips brushed hers.

Tasha rose onto her tiptoes while wrapping her arms around his neck. She loved the way he embraced her tightly. It was as if he couldn't get close enough. She felt the same way.

He tasted like coffee with a hint of bacon. She moaned while pressing harder against his body. Adam ran his hands down her back until he cupped her ass. He lifted her so Tasha brought her legs up and around his waist. He started to walk, but she didn't care where he was taking her. She simply wanted more.

"I just need to feel you for a few minutes," he whispered against her mouth.

Tasha nodded. She'd give him anything. They'd promised each other that they'd let go of their insecurities and it seemed to be working. She wanted to remind him what he was fighting so hard for. Adam deserved someone who looked out for his needs and Tasha wanted that to be her. She wanted to claim him.

It was too soon. She knew that in her mind, but she'd already begun to fall for him. Even before she'd gone to him for help finding Crystal, she'd had feelings for him. When Adam had turned out to be intelligent and kind, her heart had been lost.

Adam laid her gently on the couch but Tasha didn't release her hold on him. Instead, she pulled him down on top of her so that they were completely connected. He ran his lips down her chin and across her neck. She tilted her head to give him better access.

"You smell so good," he murmured.

Tasha laughed. "I smell like you." It was true. Adam had woken her up and she hadn't had time for a shower before he was ushering her downstairs and into the study.

"Good." It was growled.

Tasha pushed up the back of his shirt so she could get her palms on his flesh. He was hot to the touch.

"More," Adam ordered. "Touch me more."

She didn't know exactly what he needed so she scraped her nails down his back. He hissed and bucked against her. His cock was hard as he rubbed against her thigh. Oh, she needed him just as much. Growing desperate, she yanked on the back of his jeans.

A loud banging had them breaking apart.

"Fuck," Adam said, laying his forehead against hers. "I got carried away."

Tasha nodded. "Me, too."

"Whatever you're doing you need to hurry up!" Cain called through the door. "We're waiting on you."

Adam kissed her again, but this time he kept it chaste. He pulled himself up off the couch before offering his hand. Tasha placed her palm in his and allowed him to help her up.

"Sorry." He chuckled.

"I'm not," she told him. "It might not be everything I wanted, but it will get me through until we can be alone again."

"Tonight, I promise," he told her.

"You're on."

"Adam!" Cain yelled.

"I'm coming!" Adam shouted back.

"TMI," Cain teased.

"I'm gonna kill him one day," Adam said. "No one will blame me, either."

Tasha shook her head. "Come on, I'm going to see what else needs to be done for tomorrow."

"Thanks for helping," Adam told her.

"Of course." She cupped his face. "It'll be great."

"I hope so," Adam said. "I really hope so."

Chapter Eight

The smoke from the grills filled the yard as Adam and Larry fired them up. Tasha watched as her man directed the dozen Pack members who'd come early to help set up. Adam was both firm and kind as he passed out assignments.

She knew Adam was worried about the Pack being in one large group with Riker possibly out there, but he wasn't showing any stress to the others. He glanced over and caught her watching him and sent her a big smile. Tasha grinned back. He looked so good in his pressed jeans and black T-shirt. Tasha wanted to rip off his clothes, but she would have to wait until later. They would have a long evening of visiting and playing before the run. But after, once they were back in the privacy of his room, she planned on ravishing him.

"It's good to see him having a purpose," Laura said as she joined her.

"We all needed this, whether we knew it or not." Tasha accepted the red and white checkered tablecloths from Laura and set them in the chair beside her before picking the nearest up and turning to one of the tables. She flipped the covering open, letting the wind catch it, before Laura caught the other end. "He's going to be a great leader."

Laura beamed. "I know. I think I always did. Even before my dad decided that he didn't want to be Alpha anymore, I could see Adam start to grow up. He didn't see it, but the Pack had already began to come to him for some of the smaller stuff."

"I saw the same thing," Tasha said. "It was one of the reasons that I felt as though I could go to him when Crystal ran off."

"How's she doing now?" Laura asked.

"Great," Tasha said. "She called me this morning. She loves being there, but she's ready to come home. Christian and Logan are going to bring her tomorrow." Tasha glanced around before lowering her voice. "Do you think it's safe for her? I didn't tell her about Riker because I didn't want to scare her, but I'd love to have her back."

"What if we moved her into one of the guest rooms?"

Tasha jumped. She hadn't heard Adam approaching behind her. When she'd looked, he's still been talking to Larry. Damn, he moved fast. She turned. "You want to move Crystal into the Alpha house?" She was shocked.

Adam gripped her hands before pulling her away from his sister. Not that Laura couldn't listen in if she wanted to. But at least they had the illusion of privacy.

"Adam?" she whispered.

"I wanted to talk to you about it anyway," Adam stated.

"About what, exactly?"

"I know you have your own house, but I can't imagine not having you here, in my arms, every night. It's probably too soon, but I would love if you and Crystal moved in here with me." Adam shifted on his feet nervously.

She did have her own house, although she'd only been there to change clothes since her return with Adam. If she said no, once Crystal got back, she wouldn't be able to stay with him every night, not like she had been. Sure, she would be able to probably have a few overnight visits a week, but it wouldn't be the same. Was it too soon? Tasha knew what she felt for him. Adam was everything she'd ever wanted in a partner, a mate. She really wanted to say yes.

"I could talk to Crystal, ask her how she would feel about it," Tasha said.

Adam nodded. "How do you feel about it, though?"

"I want to," she confessed. "But I have to do what's right for Crystal, too."

"Yes," he agreed. "I understand."

"We'll work something out?" She didn't mean to make it sound like a question, but it did.

"Of course," Adam assured her. "I can stay a few nights with you and maybe the two of you could spend the night over here."

"I'll talk to her first," Tasha promised.

"Good." He leaned down and kissed her softly before stepping back.

Laura was watching them with a huge smile on her face. Adam slung his arm around Tasha's shoulder before drawing her back to his sister. Tasha blushed as Laura threw her arms around the two of them. "I'm so happy for you both."

"You could have waited until we told you," Adam admonished.

"I could have." Laura giggled.

"Or we could talk about your love life," Adam teased.

"Well...no..." Laura flushed while wringing her hands. "Let's not do that."

Adam walked away, chuckling.

"Let's finish setting up the tables and chairs," Tasha suggested.

"Good idea," Laura agreed.

Together they worked until all the tables were covered and the chairs were pushed in. Once they were done, Tasha stepped back to look over the area. They still needed to fetch the large tables to hold all the food, but they were going to need more help.

"What's next?" Laura asked.

Tasha pointed over to where the flattened tables were lined up. "We need to get help." Even with her shifter strength, it would take more than her and Laura to set up the tables.

"I can ask Larry," Laura suggested.

Tasha hid her smile by turning around, pretending to look for who was available. She spotted the two Council representatives talking to Larry by the drink coolers. "Good idea, maybe all three of them can help."

"Okay." Laura trotted off toward the group of men.

Instead of waiting for the help, Tasha headed over on her own. She hoped four tables would be enough. The Pack had a tendency of over-doing food when they had get-togethers.

"How's it looking?"

Tasha glanced over her shoulder to see Kurt Moore and Clint Price behind her. She'd met them both the night before, but already they reminded her of Cain. They were strong, dominant shifters but also funny and playful. She could see them getting into trouble with Cain if left on their own too long. She liked them.

"Pretty good," she replied. "Once we get these up, we can start bringing the food out. Plus, people should be showing up with their own dishes."

"Sounds good," Clint said as he bent over and flipped one of the tables. He pulled the legs up and locked them into place before spinning it back. The young blond gave a satisfied grunt as he pushed it into place.

Kurt moved to the next one and followed suit. In less than five minutes, the tables were ready for their coverings.

"Useful to have you around," Larry said, walking up with Laura.

Tasha didn't know what they two of them had been discussing, but Laura's cheeks were pink and Tasha could smell arousal coming off both shifters. She elbowed Laura, then grinned.

Larry cleared his throat. "I'll help Laura bring out the food that's ready."

"I bet you will," Clint joked.

"Shut up." Larry smacked Clint's shoulder before striding off with Laura hurrying behind him.

"Don't be a dick," Kurt said to Clint.

"I'm not!" Clint held up both his hands. "But it's pretty obvious those two are hot for each other. He just needs a little push."

"Let him be," Kurt ordered.

Clint shook his head. "You never let me have any fun."

Tasha was watching both men closely. "Do you know Larry well?"

"Pretty good." Kurt shrugged as he turned toward her. "It's no secret that the Council has had their eye on Riker's Pack for a while. Unfortunately, Riker hadn't done anything illegal that got reported, so the Council had to be careful in their investigation. We got sent in to get close to the Pack to see what we could uncover."

"The Council just couldn't stop him?" Tasha asked. She'd always wondered why Riker had been able to lead a Pack when everyone knew that he mistreated them.

"There was no proof, no accusations," Kurt said. "Only rumors."

"Oh." That saddened her.

"It was obvious to us that Larry was taking the brunt of the punishments," Kurt told her. "It just took time for him to trust us. Once he went after Brent and stopped the attacks, Riker beat him almost to death."

Tasha gasped. "Why?"

"As far as Riker was concerned, it wasn't Larry's business to help anyone other than his Pack. He stopped Cain's mate from getting hurt and she wasn't part of their family. Riker wouldn't have stepped in to save her," Kurt explained.

"That's terrible."

"Yes. If Clint hadn't heard what was happening to Larry, I don't think he would have made it. He wasn't even fighting back," Kurt said.

The back door opened and Larry stepped out, holding two platters.

"He really is a good man," Tasha whispered.

"He's perfect for this Pack," Kurt agreed. "Once we catch Riker and get him back to California, Larry will be able to move on and start a really good life here."

"I'm glad." Tasha stopped talking about the Enforcer because he and Laura were getting within hearing distance.

She hadn't seen Adam for a little while. Not since they'd had their little talk. She still couldn't believe that he actually wanted her and Crystal to move in with him. That was such a big step. They were marching forward in their relationship.

"Have you seen Adam?" she asked Laura.

"He's on his phone in the kitchen," Larry told her.

Tasha looked back toward house.

"You could grab the utensils," Laura added, giving Tasha an excuse to go check on Adam.

"Sure," Tasha said before heading in.

When she got close enough to peer through the glass door, she saw Adam leaning against the island while holding his cell up to his ear. He spotted her and grinned before gesturing her in.

She entered quietly, not wanting to disturb him.

"I really appreciate the heads-up, Austin," Adam was saying. He lifted one arm and she rushed to cuddle up to him.

Adam smelled so good and she leaned in close to nuzzle his neck. He chuckled but tilted his head so she could have better access. Adam hummed as he dropped his hand down to her waist.

She could barely hear the voice on the other end of the call and wasn't paying attention to the words. If she were brave enough, she would drop to her knees right there and see how good Adam's concentration really was. Instead, she ran her hands under his shirt and massaged his pecs. Adam leaned his elbow back on the counter and spread his legs so she could fit right up against him.

Tasha latched her mouth to the side of Adam's neck and nibbled. He bucked his hips so she trailed her hand down and cupped his erection.

"Yeah, that's helpful," Adam said, but she knew he wasn't speaking to her.

Tasha pushed up his shirt and began licking at the muscles that covered his chest. Adam gripped her hair to hold her head in place. She sucked at the skin over his heart while he continued to thrust his hips forward. She could smell his arousal, how much he wanted her.

She pulled at the button of his jeans to slip her hand inside the waistband and under his boxers. Once she had a firm hold on his cock, she stroked him.

"Uh." Adam cleared his throat. "I'll let Kurt know. Thanks again for calling." He clicked off the phone before dropping it onto the counter.

"You little minx," he accused before grabbing her around the waist and lifting her off her feet.

Tasha laughed. "What are you doing?"

"Finding somewhere we can be alone," he growled as he stalked out of the kitchen and down the hall.

His office door was open so he had no trouble carrying her through. Tasha giggled when he kicked it closed behind them. His arousal was totally intoxicating, causing her to grow even more desperate for him. Before he could get across the room, she was yanking at his shirt, trying to get it off.

"Hold on," he panted. "Almost there."

Adam dropped her onto the top of the desk, then stepped back and yanked the garment over his head before doing the same to her shirt.

"Hurry," she demanded. Tasha concentrated on undressing herself as Adam went to work on his boots.

They finished at the same time and Adam chuckled as he tossed his boxer briefs behind him. "Finally," he said, stepping between her legs.

Tasha couldn't have agreed more. Kurt and Clint had shown up late so Adam had waited up for them. Tasha had gone to bed with a kiss and a promise that he'd make it up to her. That morning, they hadn't been able to spend much quality time together since Adam had been woken up by a phone call from Cain's father, Lamont. Adam had gone downstairs so he could get coffee and let her sleep. It had been the longest that they'd gone without making love and

Tasha hated it. Just more proof that she needed to find a way to be in his arms every night.

While he nibbled on her throat, Tasha ran her palms over his ribs around to his back. She loved the way the muscles bulged under her hands.

"I need you," she whispered.

"I know." Adam slid one hand between her legs and rubbed at her pussy.

She arched, pushing her breasts up in offering. Plunging one finger inside, he sucked her nipple into his mouth. Tasha gasped as she grabbed the back of his head and lifted her hips. Even though Tasha was frantic for him, Adam always made sure she was wet and ready, too. She appreciated the caring he showed, but if he didn't hurry up, she was going to come apart before he had his cock inside her.

"Please," she begged.

Adam lifted his head before grabbing her shoulder and laying her back down on the cool wooden desk. She moaned while spreading her legs farther apart.

"That's it," he encouraged. "Open up to me."

Of course she would. Tasha would do anything, give anything, to Adam.

He gripped her hip with his free hand as he added another digit to the one that was driving her wild. He yanked her to the edge of the desk while continuing to finger her.

"Adam!" she pleaded, knowing she was so close to going over the edge.

He pulled his hand away before lifting her knees and pressing them to her chest. Tasha wrapped her arms around her own legs as he positioned the tip of his cock against her entrance.

The fierce look of determination of his face was remarkable to see, but it was the power radiating from him that had her breath catching. He was magnificent. Strong, dominant and needing her.

With his gaze locked on to hers, Adam thrust hard.

"Yes!" she hissed, accepting everything he gave her. His

girth stretched her inner muscles while at the same time the length seemed to go on forever. She was replete, filled by her gorgeous man.

"Sorry," he huffed out. "This is going to be fast and dirty."

Tasha bared her teeth, wanting the power he was displaying. "Take me."

Adam didn't hesitate. He withdrew slowly before slamming back inside. He did it again and again. The desk began to rock with their movements. She let go of her legs, using his chest to hold them in place, and lifted her arms over her head to grip the opposite side of the desk.

Sweat was beading on Adam's forehead and as much as she wanted to lick it off, she couldn't move, since she was pinned in place.

With each fast, firm drive, Adam was stealing her ability to think. All she could do was feel. She couldn't control the trembling of her legs or the shaking of her hands. It was as if she were being electrified. His to command and rule.

Tasha cried out as one more powerful thrust plunged her into an orgasm so strong her vision wavered. Adam rode her through it until all Tasha could do was collapse against the hard desk. Still, his hips didn't falter while Adam powered to his own climax.

She reached up with one weak hand to grab his forearm and dug her nails into his flesh. If she couldn't reach him with her mouth, she'd mark him any way she could.

Adam grunted before closing his eyes and drove forward one last time as she came.

His muscles of his neck bulged even as the veins stood out. His face was red and flushed while he shook hard. Tasha watched him until he stilled, then collapsed.

"Fuck," he murmured against her ear.

Now that she could reach him better, Tasha wrapped her arms around his neck and nuzzled. "Not what I had planned when I went into the kitchen, but it works for me." She was still breathless and sated but could feel her energy returning.

Adam groaned as he propped himself up on one elbow to peer down at her. "I'm glad you came and found me."

"Always," she promised. "I'll always find you."

He lowered his head and gave her the sweetest, gentlest kiss ever.

She tightened her hold, just wanting to bask for a couple more minutes.

* * * *

Adam had one hand on Larry's shoulder as he shook hands with an older male from his Pack. Larry was obviously still nervous, but the reception for Adam's Enforcer was even better than he'd imagined. Almost every single member of the Pack had shown up and all but a handful had been introduced to Larry. Maybe it was because Adam was sticking close by, or because Cain was there right at the edge giving his support, but Adam couldn't have been prouder of his Pack. They were accepting Adam's choice for his second in command. Even though most knew about Larry from him stopping Brent's attack, no one had brought that up. Instead, they'd asked about any family and how he was settling in. Adam hadn't missed the looks darting back between his Enforcer and sister and he didn't think that anyone around the two had, either.

"Mr. Washington," Adam said. "I'd like to introduce you to our new Enforcer."

"I've heard about you," Felix Washington said gruffly.

Adam stiffened. If anyone ruined the good mood around them, it would be cranky Felix Washington.

"I'm sure you have, sir," Larry replied politely. "While I can tell you not to believe everything you hear, I know it's not that simple."

"Are you a strong wolf?" Felix barked.

"Yes, sir," Larry responded.

"Can you protect this Pack?"

"Yes, sir," Larry repeated.

"And will you? Will you put every member of this Pack before yourself?" Felix pressed.

"Sir, I promise you that no one in this Pack is going to be harmed during my watch. I take my job very seriously. I don't have a family of my own any longer. I hope to find that here," Larry said.

"Call me Felix." He held his hand out to Larry, which Larry quickly accepted.

"It's very nice to meet you, Felix," Larry said.

"You, too, young man, you, too."

Felix ambled off and Adam turned to Larry. "Good job," Adam praised.

"I just spoke the truth," Larry said. "I know it will take time for people to trust me."

"Just remember that some of us already do," Adam stated.

Larry smiled. "It's actually been better than I could have expected."

"Well, remember that," Adam whispered. "Here comes Cathy Johnson. She's got hands like an octopus. Don't let her get a hold or you won't be able to shake her."

Larry laughed even as he turned toward the wild redhaired woman who approached.

"Hello, Cathy," Adam greeted.

"Alpha." She dipped her head respectfully before peering at Larry. "And who is this?"

"This is our new Enforcer," Adam introduced.

"Mmm," Cathy practically purred. "Enforcer."

"Yes, ma'am." Larry inclined his head but didn't offer his hand. "It's nice to meet you."

"Oh." Cathy latched on to Larry's arm. "The pleasure is all mine."

Someone cleared their throat and the three of them turned. Laura was standing there, glaring at Cathy.

"Alpha," Laura said. "Larry, can I speak to you both?"

"Sure," Larry answered before slipping from Cathy's hold. He did it so effortlessly that Adam knew he'd had previous experience.

Cathy huffed then stomped off while Laura was giggling softly.

"You never save me!" Adam claimed once they were alone.

"I must like Larry better," Laura quipped before dragging his Enforcer off.

Adam watched his sister and Larry stroll away arm in arm. They really did make a good-looking couple. Adam had to be careful that he stayed out of their relationship, though. He didn't want either one to feel pressured. As far as Adam knew, Laura hadn't been actively seeking out a mate. If the two found love, that would be great. If not, maybe she would be another friend that Larry could count on.

"I was looking for you."

Adam grinned as Tasha wrapped her arms around his waist from behind. When the barbecue had first started, she'd kept her distance. Every time he'd gone to her, she'd been nervous and fidgety. It had taken him a while and, okay, Larry had had to point out the fact that they hadn't been in public together yet. Once he realized that she didn't know how to act about their relationship, Adam had taken matters into his own hands.

He'd kissed her long and deep in front of the entire Pack.

The cheer that had gone up had been loud and amused.

After he'd staked his claim and let Tasha know that he was not going to hide what was happening between them, she'd loosened up. A couple of times, she'd even sought him out for a brief touch or gentle kiss.

"You found me," he replied as he turned in her embrace.

"It's almost dark." There was excitement in her voice.

"Yes," he acknowledged. "I was just about to have the little ones taken home so the rest of us could shift. I don't want to be out too late with the threat of Riker out there."

"Did we have enough babysitters?" Tasha questioned.

Adam nodded, knowing that Crystal always volunteered on full-moon runs so that the parents wouldn't have to miss out. "We currently have three females pregnant."

"Oh!" Tasha grinned. "That's great. New additions to the Pack."

More people to watch out for, to worry about and to love. It was always good to have the Pack expanding, but now that Adam was Alpha, he had to make sure their parents were taken care of and ready. Two of the three couples were expecting their first child.

That was a worry for another night, though. Tonight, they would shift and run together as family.

When a female became pregnant, she stopped shifting in order to protect the baby. Too much trauma, such as changing into a wolf, could make her miscarry. So normally the pregnant ladies of the Pack watched the other kids so that both parents could enjoy the run together.

"So." Adam shook off his thoughts. "Are you ready to shift with me in our own territory?" Adam was really looking forward to it himself. Being able to enjoy the freedom while at Gage's place had been great, but this land belonged to them.

Each blade of grass, drop of water, rock and stone was a part of them. Their scent was left behind in nature just as much as they picked up nature's aromas. This was the territory that he'd sworn to protect as well. When he ran, he always made sure to keep at least some of his attention on his surroundings where he could catalogue any areas that needed attention. He was also responsible for making sure nothing could harm his Pack.

The woods were on his private land, but that didn't mean that they never had illegal hunting or traps set. Some of those devices were absolutely barbaric.

"You're off in your own world," Tasha said, tapping his chest.

"Damn," Adam muttered. "There's just a lot on my mind."

"Anything I can help with?"

He grinned. "You can give me a kiss to give me something

else to think about."

"I guess I can do that," she teased before pushing up and against his mouth.

Adam hummed against her lips. If they weren't in public, he would have made the kiss a lot more erotic, but kids were still present, so he had to keep it clean. That didn't mean he couldn't slid his hand under her shirt and at least feel the heat of her skin.

"Alpha?"

Adam kept on kissing Tasha instead of responding to his Enforcer.

"Alpha?" Larry tried again.

"Okay, knock it off, you two." Laura smacked his shoulder.

Adam finally, slowly, pulled away from Tasha. He turned his head enough to glare at Laura.

"What?" she asked innocently.

"Um." Larry glanced between them. "The kids have been sent home and everyone is ready to gather in the clearing. Laura said she'd show me where it is. We can meet you there if you need a couple more minutes."

Adam shook his head. "Nah, it's okay. Let's go." A few minutes wouldn't be enough with Tasha and they had plans for later, anyway.

"Sure," Tasha agreed. "Let's go."

The four of them began to walk toward the small clearing located on the north side of the property. It was where special events, such as marriages and mating ceremonies, took place, plus where the Pack began a run.

"Did you check out this area on your own?" Adam asked Larry. His Enforcer had shifted the night before so he could get the lay of the land. Adam had encouraged Larry, hoping his second in command would bond with the territory all the sooner.

It would be just as important for Larry to make a connection to the land as it was for Adam. Larry needed the link so that he could protect the area and residents.

"No," Larry answered. "Hector had drawn me a map of the most-used trails and I checked them out for the run tonight. I wanted to make sure we didn't come across any surprises."

Adam approved.

"There's never been any houses built in the area," Laura said. "The first shifters who settled here thought the place held magic."

"Magic?" Larry asked.

"It's passed down that the shifters of this land were the strongest, smartest and most loyal to their Alpha in all of the US. They gathered together and chose nine to leave and become Alphas of their own territories. Rumor is that's how the Packs expanded," Laura explained.

"How do you know all this?" Tasha asked. She was holding Adam's hand, but all her attention was on Laura.

"I've always loved history. My dad let me search through every book he had, plus bringing me more from other Packs. I can spend hours studying those transcripts," Laura replied.

"That is so interesting," Tasha gushed. "I didn't know any of this."

"I keep telling Laura she should share this information with the younger Pack members," Adam said. "I think it would be great for them to carry on some of the old traditions."

"Oh, well." Laura waved her hand. "It's just something I like to play at."

"I agree with Adam," Larry told her. "I would love to hear more. I bet a lot of people would."

"Really?" Laura peered up at Larry with her big innocent eyes.

"Knowledge is power," Larry said with a grin.

"Well, maybe," Laura hedged. "If people were really interested."

"You could practice on me," Larry said.

Adam stumbled and Tasha grabbed him to keep him

from falling. Adam was still gawking at his Enforcer. That had been one bad pickup line.

"What?" Larry asked.

Holy shit, Larry was fucking blushing.

"Nothing!" Adam assured him. He glanced at Tasha.

She shook her head. "I'm not saying a thing."

"Stop teasing him," Laura demanded as she gripped Larry's elbow. "Ignore him. He might be an Alpha, but he's still immature."

"I know," Larry agreed with her.

Adam just shook his head. The two of them keep getting cuter and sweeter. Over the hill, the clearing was just in view. He could see several members of the Pack already gathered in small groups laughing and talking. He wasn't sure if he were just seeing them differently or if they were growing closer.

"Wait." Laura reached out with her free hand and tugged on his shirt.

"What?" Adam stopped walking along with Larry and Tasha.

"Just look at them," she said.

Adam glanced up. There were a few of the younger adults who were almost giddy with excitement. Some of the older members were bickering and laughing while the rest just seemed happy.

He slung his arm over Tasha's shoulder before pulling Laura close to his other side. Adam's hand brushed against Larry's back.

"They're ours and we're theirs," Adam stated firmly. "Pack."

"Pack," Larry, Laura and Tasha chimed.

"So, let's go have some fun." Adam stepped forward bringing the others with him.

One of the younger men noticed them first and started to wave.

Adam wished he hadn't waited so long to reinstate the full-moon run. Yeah, they didn't have to shift, but it had been a tradition for as long as there had been shifters in this territory.

Adam brushed his lips over Tasha's cheek before stepping into the small circle that had been formed in the dirt over the years. It was the ceremonial ring where the Alpha always stood. It was only his second time to be inside. The first being when he'd been given the Pack to take as his own.

He hadn't been alone, then, though. His father had stood by him. Now Adam was the one who had everyone's attention.

"We are strong together," he said. Adam didn't need to shout. The shifters in his Pack would hear him just fine. "Together we run tonight to pay homage to those who came before us and those who will come after," Adam continued.

"We are Pack."

"Pack!" was the resounding chant back at him.

"Shift and let us begin to bond once again."

Adam pulled his shirt over his head as an example. All around him, his Pack started to undress. He turned so he could see Tasha from where she was standing next to his sister.

Once he was naked, Adam crouched and closed his eyes. He pictured himself sprouting fur and paws and the change took him over. In minutes, he'd transformed from a human male to a strong, powerful beast.

Adam climbed onto his paws and shook his massive body before he threw his head back and howled. He called his Pack to him, telling them to come and run.

Answering cries met his ears and sent more power through him.

Tasha was small and quick as she sprinted past him. Adam let her get a good distance away before he began the chase. She was moving fast, but Adam would have no trouble running her down. He'd give it more time, though.

All around him, the rest of the Pack jogged, loped and rushed through the trees. He could hear the numerous sets of paws as they crunched over fallen leaves.

The sounds of happy howls and playful barks were splendid. It was just what he wanted to be a part of.

Ahead of him, Tasha scrambled to a stop with her nose down and tail straight in the air. Adam caught sight of the small rabbit scurrying away from Tasha. She pounced, but before she landed on the small furry animal, she changed direction.

Ah, she didn't want to actually catch anything. She just wanted to play. That gave Adam an idea. He rushed her.

Before she could react, Adam took a nip out of her flank.

Tasha reared back and snapped at him.

Adam took off running, only looking over his shoulder until Tasha started after him.

Let the games begin.

Chapter Nine

Adam laughed as he passed the coffee pot to Clint while ignoring Cain. They'd all slept in due to the late run they'd had the night before. Cain, Kurt and Clint had volunteered for guard duty so that more of the Pack could run together. Adam really owed a lot to the three men.

Now they were enjoying a calorie-filled breakfast to replenish what they'd burned last night.

Clint and Cain were picking on each other, which kept the rest of them highly amused. It was only him, Tasha, Larry, Laura, Kurt, Clint and Cain for now, but there was no telling who else might show up. Laura and Tasha had made enough pancakes, eggs, bacon and cinnamon rolls for an army. Adam took a drink of his coffee while putting his arm over the back of Tasha's chair. She leaned into him, laughing at something Laura had said.

The bonds that had started to form as soon as he'd taken over were stronger now. He'd never felt anything like this before. He could actually tell who was close by and how different people were feeling. Not everyone at the same potency. It seemed as if the more emotionally involved he was with the person, the more solid the link. He needed to talk to his dad. Adam wanted assurances that he was doing things right.

Adam's cell phone rang and he almost laughed when his father's name flashed across the screen. Tasha tilted her head back and looked at him with a furrowed brow.

"Dad," he greeted happily.

"Hello, son," Christian said. "Just calling to let you know that we're almost to the front door and we have a

135

very excited young lady who can't wait to see her sister. I wonder if she's there with you."

"Yes," he admitted. "Tasha is right here and she can't wait to see Crystal again, either. We'll meet you out front."

Tasha was already on her feet.

"See you soon, Dad." Adam rose as he turned, disconnected.

"I guess you heard," he teased Tasha.

"I know it's only been a few days, but I've missed my sister," Tasha said. She looked a little embarrassed.

"It's all right," Adam told her. "We understand."

"I can't wait to see Crystal again," Laura said. "She's one of the brightest girls I know."

"She'd love to hear more about the history of the Packs," Tasha said.

Laura nodded. "I've been thinking about what you all said last night. It might be a good idea to teach the younger shifters about where we come from."

"Let us know if you need any help," Kurt said. "The library at the Council compound is extensive. I could talk to the Council about letting you borrow some of the books."

"That would be awesome!" Laura bounced in her seat.

Adam grinned down at his sister.

A horn honked outside and Tasha squeaked.

"Let's go welcome Crystal back," he suggested.

The rest of them rose and followed them to the front door.

Christian was opening the back door for Crystal while Logan was exiting the driver side when they reached the front porch.

"Tasha!" Crystal ran to her sister who already had her arms open and welcoming.

Adam moved aside so the two women could have a private moment. He followed the others down the steps. Laura was hugging their dad so Adam met Logan in front of the hood of the SUV. They shook hands before Logan pulled him forward and pounded his back in a manly hug. Adam was both surprised and pleased. He was relieved that Logan wasn't holding Adam's first reaction about his father's relationship against him.

"It's good to see you," Adam said sincerely.

"You, too," Logan replied.

The others were gathering around so Adam turned to his father to be lifted in a giant bear hug.

"Son!" Christian exclaimed. "I'm already hearing such wonderful things about you. I'm so proud."

Adam grinned. He never got too old to hear that his father was proud of him.

"Breakfast is still warming in the kitchen," Laura said. "Are you all hungry?"

Logan nodded. "I could eat."

"If you wouldn't mind taking a walk, Adam," Christian said. "I can grab something later."

Adam glanced between Christian and Logan, but both men seemed relaxed. "Sure."

"Come on," Laura encouraged with her hand on Logan's arm. "Let's catch up."

Tasha still held Crystal, but she nodded to Adam. "I'm going to take Crystal home."

He froze. Was she leaving already? Hadn't they talked about her and Crystal staying with him? Was she even going to talk to Crystal about it?

"We'll be back for lunch," Tasha said with a wink.

"Okay." He relaxed. "We'll cook out again on the back porch." He turned to his father. "You're staying the night?"

"Yes," Christian said. "We'll leave in the morning."

"Great," Adam told him.

"See you soon," Tasha called before leading Crystal away.

Adam was alone with his father. "You wanted to walk?" he asked. He didn't know why he was nervous all of a sudden.

"Come on, son," Christian pulled Adam to the north side of the house.

He followed along, not knowing what his dad wanted to talk to him about. Christian wasn't saying anything, though, as they strolled along the side of the house out toward the clearing.

"So…" Adam drawled.

"Patience," Christian said, then chuckled.

"Right." Adam stuffed his hands in the pockets of his jeans.

The walk wasn't long and before he knew it, they were standing in front of the ceremonial circle.

"I can smell the connection between the Pack and you. You did a good thing last night," Christian said.

Adam looked around the small clearing. The different scents of the Pack members mingled with nature. It was the smell of home.

"You have the support of the Pack," Christian said. "The final phase of coming into your powers is complete."

"I wondered," Adam murmured. "It's stronger this morning."

"Yes," Christian said. "You accepted your place."

"I'd already done it," Adam said.

"No." Christian shook his head. He strode over to a fallen log and sat before motioning Adam over.

Adam huffed but followed his father. "What do you mean?"

Christian gazed out at the land that surrounded them. "You accepted the position. You agreed to be Alpha and you promised to protect everyone, but you hadn't actually joined with them. Now you have."

"I don't understand," Adam admitted.

"A true Alpha, one that this Pack needs, must do more than accept the job. You have to bond with the Pack," Christian told him.

"The run did that?" Adam asked.

"No," Christian said. "Or not just the run. It's everything combined. You became the leader you were meant to be."

"You knew this would happen?" Adam peered at his dad.

"I hoped," Christian admitted.

"You could have stayed Alpha while keeping yourself

separate from the Pack," Christian said. "A lot of Alphas do, but the Pack deserves the real connection with an Alpha."

"Why didn't you tell me this before?" Adam would have done everything he had to in order to be the best Alpha he could be.

"Because it has to come from your heart. I could have told you and you would have struggled to force it. This is something that has to happen on its own," Christian told him.

Adam sighed. There was so much more to being a good Alpha than he'd thought. He didn't know if he'd ever have things figured and now he knew his dad wasn't telling him everything. "Am I ever going to work this out?"

"You already are," Christian said.

The breeze picked up, bringing with it the sweet smell of grass. He hadn't sat out here by himself yet but he could tell this was a good space to think in. Since the area was raised, he could see pretty far. The back of the house was visible and he could see Cain and Larry working out with Hector again. Kurt, Clint, Laura and Logan sat around the large backyard table. The only ones missing were Tasha and Crystal. He didn't like the fact that he couldn't see the two young women.

Adam shifted around until he faced the section of the property where the houses and cabins were located. The trees blocked his view, but he knew where each residence was situated.

"You've also become quite close to Tasha, as well." His dad broke the silence.

"Yes," Adam admitted. "I asked her to move in. To bring Crystal and stay at the main house with me."

"I thought you might," Christian said.

"Do you think it's too soon?" he asked.

"Does it matter what I think? What anyone else thinks?" Christian questioned instead of answering.

"No," Adam told him. "She's who I want."

"In that case, it isn't too soon," Christian said. "Take it

from me. You don't want to wait years to tell her how you feel. I could have had something great with your mom and Logan. We could have figured it out. Instead, I only got a few years with the two of them sporadically. I'm trying to make it up to Logan and he's been more than understanding, but I still feel bad."

"Better late than never," Adam said. He didn't know how to make his dad feel better about it. Sure, Christian had made some mistakes, but he was correcting them. "All that matters is that you're together now."

"That's what Logan says," Christian said.

"He's a smart man," Adam said. "Maybe you should listen to him."

Christian chuckled. "Fine, and I wanted to talk about you and your girl, not my relationship, anyway."

"What about us?" Adam asked.

"I want to get to know her and Crystal better."

"You know them. They were part of your Pack," Adam pointed out.

"But I want to get to know them as part of my family," Christian said.

"Oh, wow." Adam didn't know how to respond.

"It's okay." Christian patted his shoulder. "We have time, but even though I'm not living here anymore, I just want to make sure you still talk to me."

"Always, Dad," Adam promised.

* * * *

Tasha kept her arm around her sister until they were in their own living room. She hadn't realized just how much she'd missed Crystal until she had her sister in her arms.

"I'm so glad you're home," Tasha told her.

"Me, too," Crystal said.

They were sitting beside each other on the couch and Tasha looked at her sister. Crystal had always been pretty, but now she seemed happier and that made her entire presence brighter.

"I know I said this before, but I'm really sorry about running away." Crystal reached out and placed her palm over Tasha's.

"It's forgiven," Tasha said. "Just don't ever do it again."

"I won't," Crystal promised. "But I want you to know that it's not your fault."

Tasha jerked a little. Why was Crystal even bringing this up? "It's over and we don't need to talk about it."

"I think we do," Crystal said.

"Why?"

"Because I had time to think about it. About what my running must have been like for you. I was selfish," Crystal stated.

"You're a teenager," Tasha pointed out.

"Yes," Crystal agreed. "Only a little bit younger than you when you had to start to take care of me. Well, officially, anyway."

"That's what sisters are for."

"You didn't have to," Crystal said quietly. "You were so young and had your entire future in front of you. Instead, you became my parent."

"Where's this coming from?" Tasha questioned. Crystal had never sounded so serious and it was scaring Tasha.

"Like I said." Crystal squeezed her hand. "I've been doing a lot of thinking. You grew up fast because you had to. Instead of recognizing your sacrifices, I acted like a spoiled brat."

"No," Tasha couldn't take any more of this talk. "You acted like a frightened girl who didn't understand what was going on. I wish I could have done more to help."

"But you did!" Crystal cried. "That's what I'm trying to say. I want to thank you."

Tasha scooted closer to her sister. "You don't ever have to say thank you to me. But you're welcome."

Crystal smiled. "Talking to Marissa the last couple of days really helped. She's been through a lot of what I have.

Her sister also is the only family she had before she met Gage. She helped me see that even though we're different, we're also luckier than most people in the world. Because we never stopped being loved."

"I'm glad you feel that way," Tasha said honestly.

"So." Crystal took a deep breath. "Thank you for everything you've done. Now that I'm back, I want to concentrate on helping other non-shifters like Marissa. I also want to get more involved with the Pack. I need to talk to Alpha White about what I can do."

Now would be the perfect time to being up Adam's offer to move into the main house. Tasha nervously ran her hands over the knees of her jeans.

"What?" Crystal asked. "Is he mad at me?"

"No," Tasha assured her. "He's not mad at all."

"So why do you have that weird look on your face?"

"Well." Tasha had no idea how to bring up her relationship with their Alpha.

"Is this about you sleeping with the Alpha?"

"What!" Tasha shrieked.

"Marissa helped me concentrate on my senses. I'll never be as strong or as good as a full shifter, but I've been practicing. I can smell the Alpha on you."

"Adam."

"Adam," Crystal repeated. "So, tell me about Adam. But leave out the gushy parts. I am still a teenager."

Tasha laughed. Crystal and she used to be able to have these conversations and tease each other often. It was only in the last year that they'd drifted apart. "I don't know really where to start."

"You weren't seeing him before I left, were you?" Crystal asked.

"No," Tasha assured her. "I wouldn't keep something like that from you."

"What then, you connected when you were looking for me?"

"There was always something about him," Tasha said.

"Oh, I know," Crystal teased. "I remember how you used to look at him."

"Well, it seems that he was looking at me, too. I just didn't know it."

"So you're really together?" Crystal squealed. "I'm so happy!"

"We are. In fact, there is something I need to talk to you about."

"What?" Crystal asked, frowning.

"Adam wants us to move into the main house," Tasha blurted out.

Crystal laughed. "Wow!"

"Sorry I didn't mean to just throw that out there."

Crystal nodded. "He wants us to move in?"

"Yes."

"Wow!" Crystal said again. "What are we waiting for?"

"Really?" Tasha tried not to sound too shocked. "You'd consider it?"

"Consider it?" Crystal repeated. "I'll start packing." She jumped up.

"Hold on!" Tasha grabbed her arm. "I think we need to discuss this."

"No, we don't," Crystal argued. "You want to do it. I want to do it. What is stopping us?"

Tasha had really expected needing to talk Crystal into moving. "Well, this is our house. We wouldn't have to sell it, but it's ours."

Crystal sat back down. "You mean it's where we lived with Mom and Dad?"

How in the hell did her sister get to be so smart? "It's been our home for a long time. I don't want you to think we have to leave. Adam and I can work out other arrangements."

"Why would you want to, though?" Crystal asked. "The Alpha house is awesome! He has a pool and plenty of room. There's always masses of food already made in the kitchen. We wouldn't have to live on mac and cheese."

Tasha laughed. She wasn't the best cook and they both

knew it. It was a joke between the two of them. "It might be hard on you," she said seriously. "You're already different from the other kids. I don't want you teased because of my relationship with the Alpha."

"Well, whether we move in or not, you'd still be in a relationship with him. You would just be hiding it," Crystal said. "That won't work for long. Even I know that'll lead to nothing but trouble."

Tasha shook her head. "You're right. But this is about me. It's my job to take care of you."

"I say we go," Crystal stated firmly.

"I guess we're moving!" Tasha cried.

"Yeah!" Crystal jumped back up. "This is going to be great."

"Okay," Tasha agreed. "Go pack a bag. We're supposed to be there for lunch and we can spend the night. We'll work out a schedule on getting everything else we want moved over."

"Be right back." Crystal ran toward her bedroom and Tasha had to laugh.

She hadn't expected it to be so simple. Maybe it was too easy. Things were changing fast and Tasha's head was spinning. Tasha wanted to move in with Adam, but she was just expecting something to stand in her way. Why was she expecting that, though?

Tasha stood, then strolled over to the window. She couldn't say that she really cared about leaving that house but she'd thought Crystal might. Since she'd had to step up and take care of her sister, Tasha's life had been nothing but hardship in the place. Honestly, before it was just her and Crystal, it had really always been just her and Crystal. Her parents had never been the loving, caring type. Tasha had looked out for Crystal the entire time they'd been growing up. She'd always been the one to make sure Crystal had enough to eat and clean clothes. It hadn't been a shock that in the end she was all Crystal had left.

Or she had been.

Now, they had Adam and the rest of the Pack. That was something. They were growing into a real family and Tasha should be excited, not scared.

"I'm ready!" Crystal yelled coming down the hall.

"Okay." Tasha laughed. "Let me grab a few things."

"What have you been doing?" Crystal complained.

"Nothing," Tasha said. "Just give me a few minutes." She headed toward her own room so she could pack some clean clothes. She already had some of her stuff at Adam's, but if she were going to move in, she would prefer her own toiletries. Not that she had anything against Adam's place, but his soap was a little too manly for her. Plus, it dried out her skin.

"Hurry up!" Crystal shouted. "I didn't get breakfast."

Tasha grinned. It looked as though her sister could still act like a kid sometimes.

* * * *

"I cleared out a couple of drawers," Adam said, pulling out one to show Tasha. "At least until we get your furniture over here. Or maybe we'll want to buy something new for us."

She nodded, still glancing around the room.

It was the first time they'd been alone that evening and he was weirdly nervous. He loved his section of rooms. Casual yet comfortable. He couldn't tell what Tasha thought about the space, though. She hadn't complained or commented when she'd been staying over, but now that this was going to be her home, too, he wished she'd say something.

"There's also plenty of room in the closest," he added, waving his hand over in that direction.

"Okay."

Adam spotted her bags on the end of the bed and strolled over. Cain had been the one who had brought up her stuff as he and Tasha had shown Crystal to the bedroom that would be hers.

Crystal hadn't been shy in showing her excitement. She'd practically bounced on the bed while talking at what sounded like a hundred miles a minute. Adam grabbed the closest duffel.

"I'll help you unpack," Adam offered.

"Stop," she said quietly.

Adam froze. That didn't sound good. He slowly released his hand before he turned to her. "What?"

"Just..." She stopped to take a deep breath.

Adam didn't know what else to do other than to stand there like an idiot as whatever Tasha was thinking about bothered her. Had he pushed her by asking her to move in so quickly?

"Are you sure about this?" she asked softly.

"Sure?" he questioned. "About having you and Crystal here? Of course!" He stepped forward. "Honey, I want you here, with me, every night. I want to wake up each morning and talk over coffee before we both go about our day."

"I want that, too," she said. "But if for any reason you change your mind—"

"I won't." Adam tugged Tasha against him. "I know that I won't."

Tasha nodded. "I guess I'm just a little more nervous than I thought I'd be."

"Yeah," Adam said. "Me, too."

"Really?" She sounded happy about his confession.

Adam sat on the edge of the bed and pulled her between his legs. "I've never felt this strongly about anyone before. I had a crush on you before we went looking for Crystal. It's still hard for me to believe that you share my feelings. But I'm happy. We both agreed to give this a try. I want it to work."

She leaned forward to brush her lips over his. "Thank you."

"Now," Adam said. "What should we do first? Get you moved in?"

"No." Tasha shook her head. "I think we need to christen

the bed."

He laughed. "I think we've done that."

"We did when this was your room. Now it's ours."

Adam couldn't really argue with her logic. Plus, he wanted her. It seemed as if he couldn't get enough, in fact.

Tasha grinned as she lowered to her knees. Adam watched her, his smile growing.

"Take off your shirt."

He complied quickly.

She unlaced his boots before yanking them off, along with his socks. Adam flexed his toes. Tasha was rubbing his calves while he peered down at her. Her bangs had fallen over her eyes so he brushed away the silky strands.

"Pants," she murmured.

Adam leaned back before he unsnapped his jeans and pulled down his zipper. He lifted his hips and her hands were there to help him peel off the denim. He wasn't wearing underwear and Tasha moaned in approval.

"So sexy," she said.

Adam raised his head off the mattress. She was the sexy one, sitting back on her heels while gazing up at him. Adam couldn't keep his hands off her any longer. He wrapped his hand around the back of her neck and pressed.

Tasha lowered her head as she wrapped her right hand around the base of his cock.

"Suck me," he whispered.

Her eyes flashed with arousal.

"Please." Adam needed to feel her mouth snug around his cock.

Instead of taking him deep like he wanted, Tasha licked at the head of his cock.

He grunted while bucking his hips. Adam added a little more pressure to try to convince her not to tease.

Tasha ignored his direction. She ran her tongue along his length before lapping at his balls. He jerked and grunted. *Damn, this feels good.* Tasha giggled, then did it again.

"Tasha!" he called out.

She was really lavishing his sac but ignoring his cock. He didn't want her to stop what she was doing, so Adam palmed his erection and began to stroke. She still held on to the base of his cock, but Adam was still getting good friction.

Tasha moved just behind his balls to that thin strip of flesh that was overly sensitive. She ran her finger along the skin before mouthing him.

"Jeez!" Adam cried. He sped up his hand.

"Don't come," Tasha told him. "I want to ride your cock."

He let go of himself immediately. If he hadn't, then he would have erupted at her words. "Climb on," he begged.

Tasha placed a soft kiss on the head of his shaft before clambering to her feet. "Stay right where you are."

Adam fisted his hands in the sheets while Tasha undressed. He couldn't not help. Adam started to sit up.

"If you move," she warned, "I'll play with myself and leave you there wanting."

He groaned but dropped back down. Tasha was the one in control and he was amused, aroused and frustrated.

Once naked, Tasha stepped up onto the mattress with her legs on either side of him. Adam went to reach up for her but she shook her head. Adam sighed, his shaft so hard he actually ached. Well, if she wanted to play, then Adam would have to enjoy himself, as well.

Adam licked his lips as he made sure to keep his gaze on hers. Tasha's pupils grew and her breaths came quicker. Yeah, she was going to give in.

"Come down here," he ordered.

Very slowly, she began to sink down above him. She settled on top of his thighs before grasping his cock and pumping.

"I thought you were going to ride me?"

"I am," she answered. "I'm just making sure you're ready."

Since he was already dripping with a small amount of pre-cum, it was obvious he was ready. Adam didn't hold back from moving against her hold. She smirked while stroking him but didn't say anything about him moving.

"What are you waiting for?" he growled. He was trying his best to hold back his climax, but the edge was getting closer and closer.

"That sound," Tasha said. "I love that husky sound to your voice."

Adam groaned, but finally, fucking finally, Tasha got up on her knees and scooted forward. He waited as patiently as possible as she positioned the tip of his shaft at her entrance. Adam gripped her hips before Tasha lowered herself. She did so slowly and it was absolute torture. He gritted his teeth to keep from thrusting up hard. He wanted to be buried inside her, now.

They both moaned. Adam at the feel of her soft inner muscles clamping around his cock. Tasha placed her hands on his chest before she lifted, then slammed back down. *So good.* She laughed and repeated the move. Adam could only hold on as she rode him hard and fast.

Each time Tasha plunged down, she scraped her nails across his chest. He hissed, bucked and grunted. Tasha threw back her head. She looked like a siren flowing up and down. It was the most erotic thing that he'd ever seen.

He shuddered, but that was the only movement he made. He stopped thrusting up and instead tangled his fists into the sheets and stilled his hips. The pain from being so aroused was almost unbearable. He needed to come, but he didn't want this to end.

Adam bit down hard on his lower lip.

"Okay?" she asked between pants.

"Dying," he managed.

Tasha lowered her top half down, her breasts against his chest, and kissed him hard. Adam closed his eyes even though he really wanted to watch her some more. He was just afraid that if he did, he'd come before her.

Tasha nipped at his mouth before plunging her tongue inside.

He wrapped his arms around her back before he started to drive up. He couldn't stand it any longer. Adam had to take control.

"Harder," she demanded.

Adam rolled them so she was underneath and sat back on his heels. He yanked her up by her arms so that she was sitting on his lap. In this position, he could thrust hard while she slammed down. They moved with such a smooth rhythm that Adam was having trouble catching his breath. Hell, breathing was overrated. Nothing was better than sliding in between her slick folds to claim her in the most intimate way.

"Yes," Tasha hissed. She lowered her mouth to his shoulder and bit down.

Adam roared as the orgasm rushed out of him. He was taken by surprise at the intensity. He gripped her hips, but Tasha was still riding his cock. He stayed half-hard with the pleasure coursing through his body.

When she started to mutter, he threw her back on the mattress and plowed forward over and over until she screamed.

Her climax shook her body.

Adam kept sliding in and out until she dropped back, limp.

Fuck, if they weren't careful, they were going to hurt each other.

Chapter Ten

Adam grinned at Larry before waving him on. They were taking a break for a run in their wolf forms. It had been a long day of meetings and phone calls as Adam had reached out to other Alphas, searching for any sign of Riker. Larry had gone over most of the territory with help from Cain, Kurt, Clint and Hector, but there had been no sign of anyone who wasn't supposed to be there. There was a small section up north that hadn't been explored yet. He and Larry were going to take a quick look around before dinner.

"Go," Adam called to Larry. "I'll be right behind you."

"Sure," Larry called before disappearing behind a row of trees.

Adam pulled out his cell phone and sent a quick text message to Tasha.

Meet me in our room in forty-five minutes.

He pressed Send before pocketing his cell. As he stepped under the canopy of the trees, the temperature dropped, especially when he pulled his shirt over his head. Up ahead he could hear a rustling of leaves, then a howl. Larry had already shifted. Adam undressed before rolling up his clothes and stuffing them in the base of a large oak.

Adam bent, then closed his eyes so he could concentrate on calling his wolf forward. He shuddered, then the transformation flowed over him. In a matter of minutes, he was rising onto his four paws. He gave his body a massive shake before trotting off behind Larry.

It would take less than ten minutes to get to the area and

ten back. That gave them a little time to play and run. It would be good for the two of them to bond further. Adam already trusted Larry, but he hoped Larry would feel the same way soon.

Larry was growing on the entire Pack. Just that morning Adam had spotted several of the guards smile and call out a greeting to the Enforcer. It made Adam proud of his Pack. Larry deserved the respect.

Adam howled before speeding up the trail. He could hear Larry's steady tread. He knew in a minute they would come up to the clearing marking the section they needed to survey. Larry was standing right in the middle and something was wrong. Adam slid to a stop just out of view.

Unfortunately, he hadn't been quiet. Larry didn't look in his direction, though. The fur on Larry's back and neck stood up. Adam crouched and strained to see why Larry had frozen. He didn't see anyone. He lifted his snout and breathed deeply.

The scents of nature, grass and dirt, water and animals, were all he could pick up.

He scooted forward but still remained hidden.

That was when he saw a movement in the shadows across from him. The direction that Larry was staring.

"You can come out now, Alpha," Riker said as he stepped toward Larry with a gun trained on him.

Adam mentally cursed. They had walked right up to Riker and they were alone. He hadn't actually thought they would find anything. Now he felt his failure fall like a blanket over him. By not paying attention, he'd put his Enforcer in danger.

"I said, come out!" Riker yelled.

Riker looked rougher than Adam remembered. His dark hair was longer and appeared stringy. He was dirty and Adam wondered if he were closer, if he'd been able to smell the stink from Riker.

Larry lowered his belly onto the ground and Riker laughed. "Go ahead and shift," Riker taunted. "You always were a coward. Could never take me on."

Adam snarled. He didn't like Riker talking to Larry that way. What worried him even more was that Larry had laid his chin on his paws in submission. It seemed just so wrong.

He didn't have a choice. Adam pushed at his wolf and pictured his human form. The transformation came quickly before Adam stood on shaky legs. Two shifts so close together was not going to help him beat Riker, but Adam was an Alpha and he wouldn't allow Larry to be hurt.

Riker was close enough to Larry that if Larry lunged, he would get a good bite, but he'd also get shot. Adam stepped out into the open, which gained him Riker's attention. The gun was now pointed at him. At least Larry was safe for the moment.

"Come on, Alpha," Riker sing-songed. "You have a lot to answer for."

"Really?" Adam crossed his arms over his chest. He ignored the fact that he was naked going up against an armed man. "And what would that be?"

Riker waved the gun in Larry's direction, making Adam tense. "You took in this traitor!"

"Traitor?" Adam repeated slowly. "You're the only traitor I see here. You were an Alpha. It was your job to protect your Pack."

"I had the strongest Pack in all of the States," Riker hollered. "If this weakling hadn't turned the rest of the Pack against me, I would still be in charge, on my way to leading the Council."

Adam barked out a laugh. He needed to keep Riker's attention on him. "You would never be on the Council. Crazy is easy to see when it's close by. You might have been able to hide in your own territory but—"

"I was a god!" Riker yelled angrily.

Shit, Riker really had lost his fucking mind. He was unhinged and they were in real danger. As Adam spoke, he moved closer to the man and wolf in the middle of the clearing. Riker was so far gone he hadn't even noticed.

"And after I deal with the two of you, I will take over your Pack," Riker told him. "They will bow to my will. I'll take the strongest and we'll wipe out the weak."

"All you're going to do is face the Council for crimes against your Pack," Adam said.

Riker cackled. "Who's going to turn me in? You?"

"Yes," Adam said sincerely.

Riker pointed the gun back at Larry. "Don't come any closer, or I'll shoot him."

Adam followed his gaze to see that Larry hadn't moved at all. Riker was aiming for his head. Larry wouldn't be able to recover. What could he say to get Riker's attention back on him?

"You're a disgrace," Adam said with true revulsion.

"What do you know?" Riker asked. "You've been an Alpha for what? Five minutes? You know nothing about leading a Pack."

"I know not to abuse them," Adam retorted. He was relieved when Riker faced him and the weapon was no longer above Larry.

"Abuse?" Riker repeated. "I made them strong."

"You got off on their pain," Adam said. "You're one sick puppy." Three more steps closer.

Riker's face was red but his hand was steady. Adam needed to throw him off. He turned his head slightly but made sure Riker would see him. He peered into the woods and let a small smirk show. If he could convince Riker that he wasn't alone, maybe he could get the upper hand.

Just as he'd planned, Riker's gaze swung nervously between him and the spot where Adam had looked.

"What's your plan?" Adam asked. "You shoot us both?"

"Sounds good to me," Riker responded.

"You can't take over my Pack that way," Adam told him.

"What do you mean?" Riker seemed honestly confused.

"I have a back-up Alpha," he said.

Riker glanced at Larry.

"Not him," Adam lied. "Why do you think Cain is here?"

"Cain?" Riker repeated. "He already has a Pack."

"But he'll never be Alpha there," Adam pointed out. "Tony will take over the Pack once Lamont retires or goes to the Council. After that, Toby will be old enough. Cain will never lead that Pack. Here he has a chance." It was complete bullshit. Cain didn't want to be Alpha. If he did, Lamont would have no issues leaving the Pack in his hands, but Riker didn't know that.

"I'll kill him, too," Riker said, but he sounded a lot less sure.

"No, you won't," Adam assured him. "Once Larry and I go missing or are killed, Cain will be on alert. You'll never get close enough to get the drop on him."

Riker narrowed his eyes. "Well, at least I'll get rid of the two of you. Then I'll move across the country and find my own Pack again."

"No," Adam said. "You'll never lead again." He launched himself at Riker. Riker cried out in surprise before bringing up his arm. The gun went off, but Adam was prepared and hit him in the side before he could aim. The bullet hit the dirt several feet away from where they landed on the ground.

"No!" Riker howled.

Adam punched Riker hard in the face. Riker's head fell back before he growled and clamped his teeth into Adam's arm. Adam cried out as he grabbed the back of Riker's hair and yanked.

They rolled, each trying to get the upper hand. A low whimpering reached him and Adam knew it was Larry who was now up on his feet, pacing in his wolf form.

Adam couldn't worry about his Enforcer, though. Riker was desperately trying to claw at Adam's hand. Riker wrapped his legs around Riker's waist, gaining the advantage. He was straddling Riker, bringing his arm back to try to knock him out when Riker started to change under him.

No, no, no. If Riker shifted, then he would be able to

handle Adam easily. Adam pushed Riker away from him and began his own shift. It hurt, which was unusual, but expected, since this was his third one in such a short time.

It also took longer that it would normally.

His eyes were closed, but he could hear that Riker had finished shifting. He willed his transformation to complete faster. He was vulnerable. Adam prepared himself to be attacked. Instead, there was a growl and the sound of a fight. Fear made his change even more painful. This wasn't good. Adam stumbled when he tried to take a step. His vision swam.

A sharp yelp.

He forced his body to settle. Once the shaking stopped, Adam opened his eyes and saw Larry standing in front of him, protecting him from Riker. Riker was barking and lunging and while fear was radiating off his Enforcer, Larry was not letting Riker anywhere near Adam.

Adam knew Larry was scared because of the abuse he'd endured at Riker's hands, but the fact that Larry was still protecting his Alpha made Adam pleased. Pride filled him and gave him the strength that he needed to push back the exhaustion of shifting.

He growled before stalking toward Riker. Adam was the Alpha of this territory and he was going to show Riker why. Riker had made a mistake coming onto Adam's land to hurt his Enforcer. Adam threw back his head and howled. He was warning Riker while at the same time calling the rest of his Pack.

Riker stumbled as Adam's cry rose and Adam's dominance soaked the area around them. With his fangs in full view, Adam leaped over Larry and faced off against Riker. Riker was a smaller wolf than Adam and looked sick and thin. Adam was almost positive that Riker used to be much larger.

Riker spat and foamed as he continued to snap, but Adam wasn't afraid. Larry stepped up to his side and bared his own teeth at Riker. Riker's attention went straight to Larry once again. Even though Adam was the bigger threat, Riker obviously wasn't thinking straight since he swiped at Larry. Adam circled Riker, looking for the perfect opening. Riker was so intent on getting a piece of Larry that Adam was able to get behind him.

Larry growled while charging and retreating, keeping Riker's full interest. Every once in a while, Larry would look over at Adam to make sure he was doing what his Alpha wanted. Adam nodded back to his Enforcer. Riker caught Larry's shoulder with a wide swing of his claws. Larry yelped before scrambling away.

Enough was enough. Adam timed it perfectly so that when Riker jumped at Larry, Adam leaped on Riker's back. He threw Riker off balance so that the old Alpha fell and had to scramble up before Adam could pin him. Fatigue threatened to make him collapse, but he had to keep his eye on Riker as the two of them continued to snap and snarl at each other. Adam had lost sight of Larry, but that was okay because it also meant that Larry was out of harm's way. Adam now had all Riker's attention.

Riker darted his gaze around, seemingly unable to focus.

Was he going to run? Oh, hell no, Adam wasn't going to let Riker get away. He didn't want to kill the old Alpha, but Riker was going to get sent to the Council so he could be held responsible for his actions.

Adam dove at Riker's legs and had the older Alpha rolling. Adam followed along until Riker stopped on his back. Adam jumped him and buried his teeth into Riker's soft throat. It wasn't a kill strike, but it would hold Riker down until the older Alpha gave up.

Out of the corner of his eye, he could see Larry step up in front of Riker's head to take a protective stance.

Riker was still fighting, but one shake of Adam's head had his fangs going deeper and Riker whimpered.

The sound of thundering paws on the ground reached him and he could smell other wolves approaching. He picked up on Cain's frantic breaths before his best friend was at his side and growling above him and Riker.

Riker went limp, obviously knowing he was beaten.

"Everyone okay?"

It was Kurt's strong deep voice that had Adam relaxing. More back-up had arrived, and apparently, some were shifting back to human form. Adam wasn't sure if he'd even be able to at this point. Adrenaline still coursed through his body and he'd already been pushing himself.

"We'll take it from here," Kurt said, placing his palm on the back of Adam's neck.

Adam released his hold on Riker but growled into the old Alpha's face before he backed away. He looked around and saw Kurt and Clint naked and in human form while another three male wolves were circling them. His Pack and friends had heard his call and come running.

There were more sounds heading toward them and Adam faced that direction.

Tasha soared into the area, looking frightened and determined. Adam wanted to go to her and reassure Tasha that he was okay, but his legs were shaking too badly. She spotted him and hurried over. Tasha nosed at his neck and snout before rubbing against his flank. She was trying to comfort him, but it wasn't Adam who needed the care. He looked over his shoulder at Larry, but Cain was already there. Cain had shifted and was running his hands over the wounds Larry had sustained.

"He's okay," Cain called when he noticed Adam watching. "When he shifts back, he'll be healed up."

Larry lowered his belly to the ground and he looked so defeated that Adam couldn't stop himself from going to him. A cramp in his side had him biting back a wince, but he couldn't worry about himself right then. He needed to check on his Enforcer.

Tasha, however, stayed plastered against him and her silent support gave him the strength he needed. Larry met Adam's gaze as he approached. Adam bent down and licked at Larry's muzzle. Larry whined before rolling over onto his back and exposing his vulnerable belly in submission. Adam didn't want Larry's surrender, though. Adam was proud of his Enforcer. Not only had Larry protected Adam during his shift, but Larry had stood up to the bully who had tormented him for years.

Having no other choice so he could talk to his Enforcer, Adam called forward his transformation. Long minutes went by before Adam sat in the clearing naked and panting.

"Here." Tasha handed him a bottle of water. "Take small sips."

He nodded before bringing the plastic bottle to his mouth and taking a drink. The cool, refreshing liquid soothed his sore throat. Adam glanced over his shoulder and saw Tasha crouching beside him. She'd finished her shift before him so it made him wonder just how long it had taken him. He frowned when he noticed she was naked.

"I've got some clothes," Laura announced as she walked out of the woods carrying a couple of backpacks.

"Get dressed," Adam ordered her in a rough voice.

Tasha laughed. "Yes, sir," she said, amused.

He glowered but she only bounded off with a sexy sway of her hips. Adam turned his attention back to Larry, who hadn't moved. Adam placed his hands on Larry's stomach and rubbed.

"I'm so proud of you," Adam whispered.

Larry whimpered as he shook his head.

"Yes," Adam said firmly. "You protected me and made sure Riker couldn't get to me until I shifted." Larry licked his hand. "Even though you were scared, you still did your job. We're very lucky to have you with us."

Another sharp sound came from Larry.

"It's okay," Adam soothed his Enforcer. "Can you shift back?"

Larry flipped over to his stomach before he began to change back to human. Adam waited patiently until Larry was naked in front of him, once again human.

"You okay?" Adam asked him.

"Yeah, sure," Larry said unconvincingly.

Riker shouted and they both glanced over. Kurt had forced the old Alpha back to human form and Clint was yanking him up to his feet. Kurt and Clint had dressed and Clint had a pair of handcuffs ready. Larry had stiffened at the sound of Riker, but Adam placed his hand on Larry's shoulder until his Enforcer calmed.

"Sorry," Larry said quietly as he moved closer to Adam.

"There's nothing to be sorry about," Adam said.

"There is," Larry insisted. "He came after you because of me." Larry blushed. "I froze, I couldn't move, couldn't fight him."

"Yes, you did," Adam said. "You stood between me and Riker. That was your job and you did it."

"No." Larry shook his head. "I failed you and the Pack."

Adam sighed. "How?" he demanded. He didn't know what he needed to say to get through to Larry. "We knew Riker could be here and you accompanied me to check this part of the territory. Together we took care of him until back-up arrived. How did you fail us?"

Larry opened his mouth to reply but didn't say anything.

Adam lifted an eyebrow.

A soft chuckle escaped from Larry. "I don't know," he confessed.

"That's what I thought," Adam patted Larry's back. He could see Laura hanging close by with two stacks of clothes and knew that his sister wanted to check on Larry herself. "We'll talk more later on, but all you need to know right now is that I'm proud of you." Adam stood. "We'd better get dressed and help Kurt and Clint get Riker back to the house."

"The house?" Larry repeated as he paled.

Shit, Adam hadn't thought about what they were going to do with Riker until Kurt and Clint left. He couldn't ask them to leave tonight when it would put them on the road late.

"What about my place?" Tasha suggested, returning to

his side.

"What?" Adam asked surprised.

"Him." She waved a hand at Riker. "We could put him at my house with guards. It's away from the main house but not so far that you couldn't get there fast if there was an issue."

Adam nodded. It was a good idea. He twined his fingers with Tasha's and gave her a squeeze as he glanced over at Cain. Cain nodded before he stalked over to Riker and yanked the old Alpha forward. Kurt and Clint flanked him as they started down toward the houses.

"Thanks," Larry said quietly.

"Of course," Adam responded.

"What do you want us to do?" Hector asked as he and James joined them.

Adam looked at James. "Three guards on four-hour shifts. One must be in the same room with Riker at all times."

James nodded. "I can do that part. Four additional guards, two inside and two out. We'll give Kurt and Clint time to eat and sleep so that they can leave in the morning if that's what they want."

He approved and told James so. "I want Hector at the main house," Adam added.

Hector's head snapped up. "Alpha?"

"You have a very important job," Adam told him.

"I do?" Hector asked suspiciously.

"We're on high alert," Adam said. "I don't think that Riker had any help, but we can't take the chance that he's not alone. That's why I want the extra guards on him."

"I could help," Hector offered. "I'm getting better at fighting."

"I know," Adam said. "That's why you're in charge of the protection for Tasha and Crystal."

Hector's eyes grew wide. "Me?" He glanced between Adam and Tasha. "But they're…they're yours."

"Yes," Adam agreed. "They are."

"There's others that are better at—"

"No one has shown as much initiative as you. You don't want the job because of the money or position, but because it's what you were meant to be," Adam said.

"It's all I ever wanted," Hector confessed.

Adam smiled at him. "That's how I know you won't let me down."

"I won't!" Hector promised.

James was chuckling along with Adam. "Come on, bud," James threw his arm around Hector's shoulder. "You can help me call in the other guards."

"Sure," Hector agreed, practically bouncing as James led him away.

"That was nice," Tasha said, leaning against him.

"And smart," Larry added. "He really will take his job seriously."

"Yeah," Adam agreed distractedly. He peered around the clearing. They didn't come up there often, since it was far away from the trails the Pack normally ran. Adam knew how lucky they were that Riker hadn't hurt anyone. That they'd come across him before he could touch any Pack member.

"We'll meet you back at the house," Laura said, pulling on Larry's hand.

Larry waited until Adam nodded before he followed along.

"What's wrong?" Tasha asked once they were alone.

"Nothing." Adam shook his head. Now that everyone had left, he didn't know if he had the energy to make it to the house. "I'm just tired."

"I bet," she said softly.

Adam nuzzled her cheek. "You shouldn't have come up here." They were going to have to talk about her putting herself in danger.

Tasha laughed. "Yeah, sure."

He didn't roll his eyes, although he did feel the need. It didn't surprise him that she was blowing off his concern. "I mean it," he said.

"When I heard you howl, there was no way that I couldn't come," she said, seriously.

He sighed. Adam hadn't even considered she would have heard his call along with the rest of the Pack.

"Besides, I stayed behind the others. I could have passed them easily enough."

She *was* fast. "At least that's something."

Tasha moved in front of Adam and cupped his face. "I'm so glad you're okay."

Adam smiled. "I was never in any real danger." He didn't need to tell her about the chance of Riker attacking him during his shift. "Besides, I had Larry with me."

"Thank goodness," she murmured. "I'm glad this is over for him, as well."

"Me, too," Adam agreed. "Now we can concentrate all our attention on the Pack and making sure everyone is healthy and happy." It would be nice to finally have the time to finish putting his inner circle together and care for those in his Pack. "Let's head back to the house. I want a shower and food before I check in with Kurt and Clint. I also want to call Alpha Winters and let him know that Riker has been caught. Austin has had a lot of worry on his shoulders, as well."

"That's the Alpha who took in Riker's Pack?"

"Yes," he answered. "Austin's Pack grew quite a bit in a short amount of time and he didn't need the added burden of Riker's threat."

"I hope Riker pays for all he's done."

"He will." Adam was certain and made sure his tone showed the confidence he had in the Council.

Adam looked around the area one last time. Maybe they needed to do something special with the spot. Ideas sprang to mind and he grew excited. There were quite a few teenagers in the Pack as well as some kids about to reach that age. The younger children had a playground, but the teens didn't have anywhere they could hang out just for fun.

The clearing was large enough for a soccer field or something. Plus, they could haul up some furniture and make it nice. The distance from the houses would make it ideal for loud music. Of course the area would be monitored and guarded because they were talking about teens, but Adam thought they did need some place just for themselves. He'd have to ask Crystal what she thought about the idea.

"What are you smiling about?" Tasha asked with a furrowed brow.

Adam kissed her. "Tell you later. Let's go."

"Okay." She slipped her hand back in his.

As they stepped under the canopy of leaves and large trees, the temperature dropped but the birds above them began to sing. It was beautiful. Adam fucking loved his territory.

* * * *

Adam rinsed the shampoo out of his hair before shaking his head. It felt good to be clean and the stress of the day had left him as though he'd washed it down the drain.

"Hey."

He turned his head and saw Tasha standing outside the shower stall, holding a towel for him. Adam smiled at her.

"Crystal go to bed?" he asked. Crystal had been frightened by Riker's appearance, but he and Tasha had managed to get her settled.

Once they'd returned to the main house, they'd found Crystal pacing the back porch while Larry and Laura had tried to reassure her that he was okay. It wasn't until Crystal had spotted him and ran over to throw her arms around his neck that the teen had really believed he was unharmed. During dinner, Crystal hadn't strayed too far from him, so after they'd eaten he'd taken her for a walk and brought up his plans for the land where they'd been earlier.

Crystal had loved the idea of the teens having a place

to hang out that was still inside the territory so they'd be safe but could listen to music and relax. He'd given her the task of contacting some of the other teenagers in the Pack to come up with ideas for the space. They were growing closer and Adam was beginning to think of her as his own little sister, not just Tasha's.

"She did," Tasha answered his question. "She called every shifter in her high school tonight. You might have a full house in the morning if Crystal gets her way. They want to start right away."

Adam nodded while washing the rest of the soap from his body. Once he was clean, he shut off the taps before sliding open the door. Tasha handed him the towel and he took it, quickly wiping off the water. "I suspected. I'm glad Crystal liked the idea."

She waited until he'd wrapped the towel around his waist before she stepped up and wrapped her arms around his neck. "You're such a good Alpha."

"Am I?" he asked.

"Yes," she said. "But you're an even better boyfriend."

He grinned. "Boyfriend?" He repeated the word but it didn't sound right on his tongue. Boyfriend wasn't a strong enough term for what he felt for her.

"Boyfriend, partner, lover." Tasha placed kisses over his naked chest as she spoke. "Whatever you want to be called."

Adam placed his hands on her shoulders to still her. "What about mate?"

Tasha stiffened before she peered up at him. Her eyes were wide and she looked scared. Adam frowned. He was certain Tasha felt the exact same way for him as he did her. He grasped her chin before his thumb and finger so she couldn't look away.

"What did you say?" she asked quietly.

"I asked if you'd ever consider mating with me."

"Consider?" she repeated.

"I know you probably think it's too soon—"

"No!" Tasha cried.

Adam's stomach rolled. He hadn't even considered she wouldn't want to make their relationship permanent. "Oh."

"It might be too soon, but I don't care," she hurried on. "I want to."

"Why?" He didn't know how to phrase his question.

"You surprised me," she explained. "I keep waiting for you to notice one of the other women who watch you. Once you mate with me, I'll never let you go."

"I'll never let you go whether we mate or not," Adam said. "But I want to claim you. I want you to wear my mark and for me to wear yours."

"Adam." She murmured his name as she put her forehead on his shoulder.

"I love you," he confessed. He'd never told any person outside his family that.

"I love you, too," she whispered.

Adam ran his palm up and down her back. "I don't look at the other women in the Pack, because they're not you. It's you I want."

Tasha peeped up at him with tears in her eyes. "I can't believe you want to mate with me."

He kissed her gently. "You're mine now. We'll spend the next couple of months taking care of our Pack, but while we do that, we'll plan a ceremony fit for an Alpha and his wonderful mate."

Tasha's smile lit up her entire face. She laughed before jumping up into his arms. Adam caught her easily with his hands under her ass while she attacked his mouth. She nipped at his lips as she squirmed against him.

The towel around his waist fell to the ground, but he didn't care. He walked out of the bathroom and into the room they now shared. All around, he could see little additions of Tasha's that made the entire space theirs.

Her shoes were kicked off beside the bed. On the nightstand sat her keys and phone along with a mystery book she read when they were settled in for the night.

She wouldn't be reading that evening, though. Adam was going to claim her the only way he could until they had the ceremony that would bind them together.

Adam laid her gently on the mattress before he stood over her and slowly undressed her. Her cheeks were flushed and her breathing fast. *God, what a fucking beautiful vision.*

"Hurry!" she pleaded. "I need to feel you."

"Play with yourself," he demanded. Watching her tease and prepare herself for him was one of Adam's favorite sights.

Tasha didn't hesitate, trailing one hand between her thighs while cupping her breasts with the other. As he began to pump two fingers inside her sweet, tight pussy, Adam grasped his cock and stroked. He wanted to come all over her body. To mark her with his seed and not allow her to shower so that every shifter could smell him on her skin.

He hadn't managed to do it, since anytime he got close, he had to be buried deep inside her. But one day he was going to follow through.

"So good," Tasha murmured. She was lifting her hips and really riding her own hand as he sped up his own pace.

"I'm going to come if I keep watching you," he told her.

Tasha pulled her hand away before spreading her legs. "Get over here. I want to be filled by your huge cock."

He grinned then climbed up on the mattress between her thighs. He was still gripping his shaft and positioned himself to push inside. Adam took his time, resisting the urge to thrust hard. He wanted to savor this moment. It was the first coupling since Tasha had agreed to mate with him and after they'd said they loved each other.

"I love you," Tasha said the words right then and he almost came. Instead, he clenched this teeth while driving forward. He had to make this memorable for her, as well.

"Love you," he told her before he withdrew, then plunged.

Their gazes remained locked as Adam continued to claim her body. Tasha ran her hands over his back, her touch sending tingles down his spine. He didn't know if he'd ever get enough of the feel of her tight inner muscles clamping around his cock and really hoped he didn't. She was so perfect for him.

"Adam!" Tasha cried out his name as she climaxed.

Adam kept thrusting, grasping her hands with his, until he came with a shout.

He couldn't hold himself up and barely had time to pull out before his arms began to shake. Adam did manage to fall to the side instead of on top of her. The exhaustion that he'd felt earlier was back and now that his body was sated, he couldn't even clean them up.

Tasha was caressing his side, but then she shifted on the bed. "Climb up here and hold me," she said.

It took the remaining energy he had, but they moved up to the head of the bed and cuddled under the sheets. As they settled in, Adam rubbed his chin over the top of her head. The balcony doors were cracked open and he could hear the sounds of his territory as he lay there.

He was happier than he could ever remember being. His life was about as perfect as he could have ever hoped for. Adam smiled as he closed his eyes and let the scents and sounds of his territory follow him into sleep.

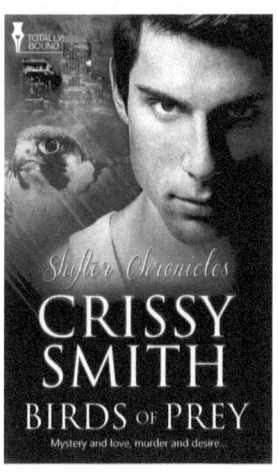

Birds of Prey

Excerpt

Chapter One

The call came at five in the morning.

Cody fumbled on the nightstand beside his bed and knocked something onto the ground as he reached for his cell phone. "Hello?"

"Agent Johnson," Commander Jacob Green's brisk voice came through loudly.

"Yes, sir?" Cody replied with a wince. It was Sunday and his day off. He'd gone out the night before with Zak and Jamie and had only climbed into bed three hours ago. Sadly, he'd crawled into bed alone but with too much alcohol in his system. If he was being called in, a hangover was not going to help.

"I need you and your team to report to a scene," his boss told him.

Cody sat up and rubbed his hand roughly over his face.

"Okay." It wasn't normal procedure to call in one of the teams that wasn't on the schedule. His superior had also never phoned him personally before.

"I'll text you the address," Commander Green said, lowering his voice. "It's going to be a long day."

"Understood, sir," Cody replied, before his boss disconnected the call. Even if he didn't understand yet, he wasn't going to argue with his employer.

He only had to wait a few seconds for the address to be sent to his phone. And that was all he got.

1125 Lake Shore Drive.

No names or information on what he and his team would be walking into. Not normal at all.

He forwarded the text with the addition to report ASAP to his unit.

Swinging his legs over the edge of the bed, he couldn't hold back a groan. He should have known better than try to match shots with Jamie, but the bear shifter had kept pushing.

Zak had just laughed at them as they threw back round after round.

It wasn't the first time he'd made the mistake of trying to take his buddy on and it probably wouldn't be the last.

Cody needed coffee. Strong and black, and a lot of it.

He walked to his closet and pulled out a clean pair of jeans and a black T-shirt. He tossed them on the bed as he crossed to his dresser. He yanked out a pair of boxers and socks. His boots were still right next to the bed where he'd kicked them off earlier.

Dressing quickly in what he considered his daily uniform—jeans, shirt and boots—he was once again glad that he was part of a field team and rarely had to put on a suit. He preferred to be comfortable when he worked.

Picking up his cell again, he noted that all three members of his crew had replied affirmatively, just as he had expected.

He strolled out of the bedroom and down the hall of his two-bedroom, one-bath apartment. He didn't bother turning on any lights until he reached the kitchen.

There, he flipped on the switch above the sink to light up the room then pulled his travel cup from the cabinet above his single-serve coffeemaker.

He put in the strongest blend and started up the machine. Sixty seconds later, the aroma of the strong brew almost caused him to weep in relief.

Once his coffee was finished, he placed the lid on tightly and headed out. He grabbed his badge, wallet and keys from the side table by the front entrance just before he unlocked and opened the door.

Outside, it was already reaching the high eighties and he knew it would only get hotter as the day wore on. It wasn't even light yet, and the dry air was already stifling.

Didn't matter, he mused. Something had happened and he suspected that it wouldn't be just a long day, but a long *few* days.

He climbed into his old Jeep and started it up. The air conditioner blasted on, sending warm air into his face. He cursed and wrenched the knob to low.

Before he backed out of his parking place, he typed the address into his phone's GPS and waited. Once the GPS announced the route he should take, he shifted into reverse and drove to work.

It took him twenty minutes to reach Lake Shore Drive. The street was located in the classy part of town. Old money. Big money. No wonder Commander Green had called him in personally.

This was going to be high profile.

Damn, that meant media and gawkers.

He hated that.

And since it was his unit that had been assigned, a bird shifter would be involved in some way.

He turned onto the quiet street, admiring the large houses. This neighborhood was made up of two and three-story structures that spread onto perfectly manicured plots. Even though he'd grown up in Lake Worth, he had never spent a lot of time in this area of the city.

Two blocks down the street, he finally saw the lights from police cars. His GPS announced that he was coming up on his destination. He reached over and turned the program off.

Roadblocks had already been placed limiting access, so Cody had to pull off to the side. He exited his vehicle and made sure that his badge hung in view from around his neck.

City cops roamed about or stood in small groups as Cody stepped around the barricades. He narrowed his gaze as he took in the scene.

Tall, wide iron gates stood open with a ruined vehicle still smoking just inside.

Plainclothes detectives were speaking with his boss. He headed over there first.

Yellow crime tape roped off the smoldering SUV, preventing anyone from gaining access.

"Here he is now." Commander Green waved him forward.

Cody joined the three men.

"Detectives Lawrence and Sanchez, this is Agent Johnson," Commander Green introduced.

Cody shook each of the detectives' hands. Their grips were firm but not aggressive.

"Agent Johnson, it seems this scene will be turned over to you," Detective Sanchez said. He was obviously unhappy with that decision, if his scowl was anything to go by.

More books from Crissy Smith

Book one in the Were Chronicles series

Marissa Boyd finds herself drawn into a world she can never be a part of, complete with an Alpha wolf who takes whatever he wants. And he wants her.

Book one in the Bloodlines series

If trouble doesn't come to him, he'll find it on his own.

TOTALLY BOUND *What's her Secret?*

Piper's Happily Ever After
had been postponed...

*Designated
Alpha*

CRISSY
SMITH

Part of the What's her Secret? collection

*Piper's happily ever after has been postponed. Destiny is
funny like that.*

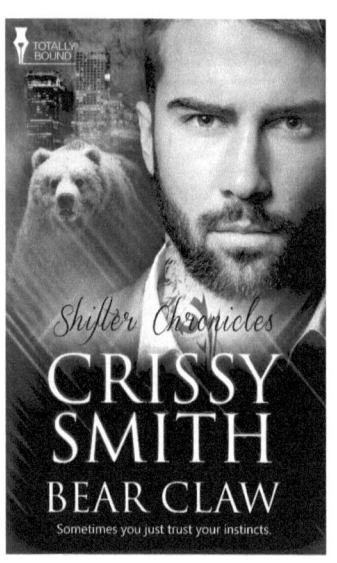

Book two in the Shifter Chronicles series

Beauty and grace meet muscles and tattoos. When what's on the outside doesn't match the inside, sometimes you just trust your instincts.

About the Author

Crissy Smith

Crissy Smith lives in Texas with her husband, daughter, and three Labrador retrievers. The three dogs love to curl up under her computer desk and nap while she writes. It doesn't leave a lot of room for her but what's a woman to do?

When not writing or reading, she enjoys hunting, camping and shooting. But she has a girly side too and is addicted to pedicures and coffee.

She has been writing since she was a teenager and still loves everything to do with the paranormal. Her stories and characters all have a place in her heart. She loves the alpha male, the dominant werewolf, or the Master vampire which find their way in most of her books.

Learn more about the characters she has created at her website where they have their very own page. It will be updated from time to time to let you know what's going on with them. Also you can find out who will be in the next book.

Crissy Smith loves to hear from readers. You can find contact information, website details and an author profile page at https://www.totallybound.com/